GHOST OF TOMORROW

GHOST OF TOMORROW

MAYA RUSHING WALKER

Published by Apollo Grannus Books LLC www.apollogrannus.com

Cover design by Streetlight Graphics, *www.streetlightgraphics.com*

ISBN: 978-1-953613-05-9

www.mayarushingwalker.net

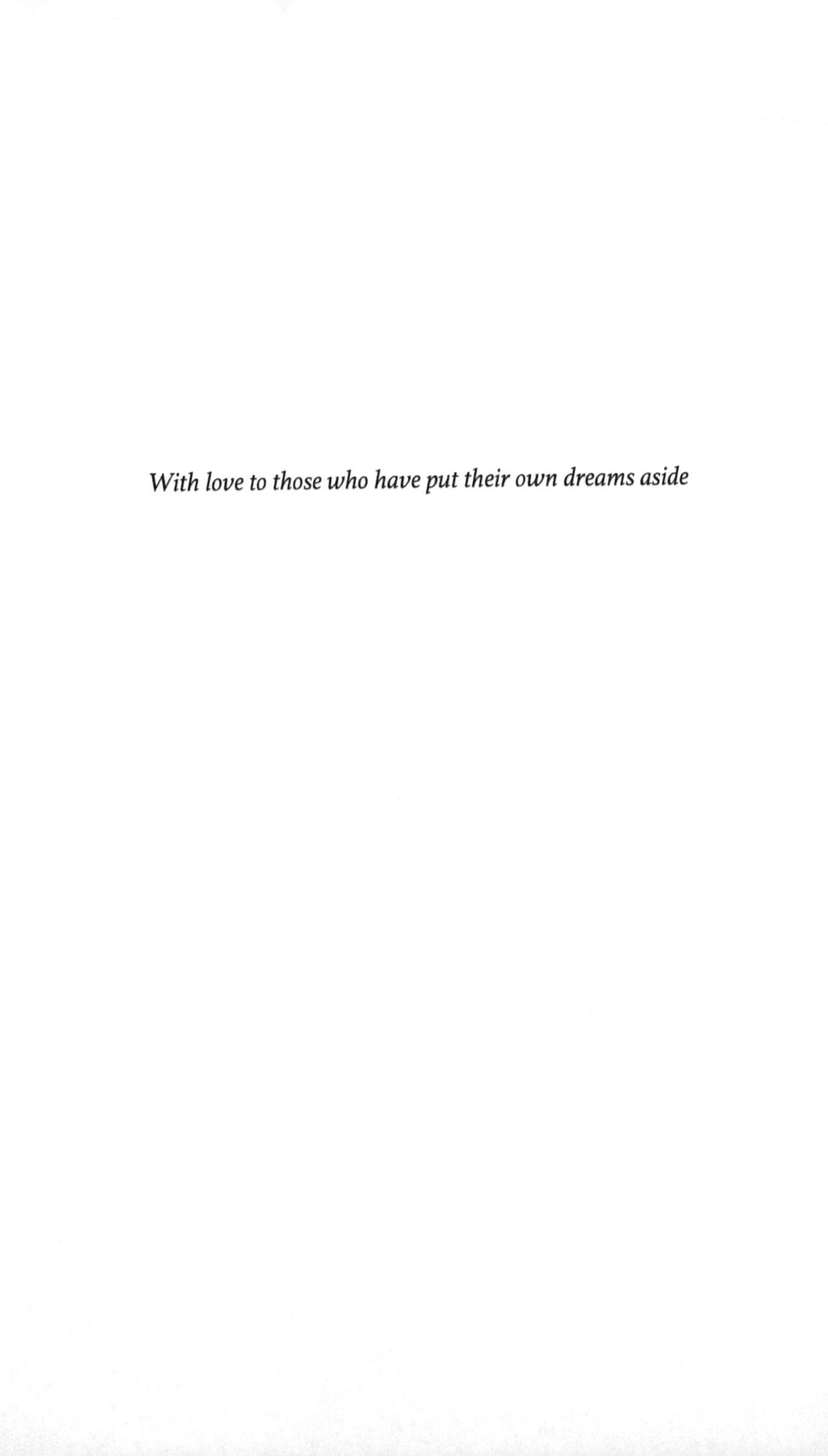

With love to those who have put their own dreams aside

1

January cold. Not like December cold. Not like February cold. Brutal, bone-chilling, unrelenting. Single digit air temps. Negative wind chill. Scarf weather, for sure. And ears get frostbitten first, so skipping the scarf, even for a quick saunter across the yard, is not a good plan. As they say in Scandinavia, there's no such thing as bad weather, just bad clothes. The weather—it just is what it is, and will be.

One thing about cold is that it wanders. It doesn't stay still. Through the magic of physics, cold air moves into places where it shouldn't, finding the cracks in window casings and storm doors that won't pull tight. And once it gets in, hell if you'll manage to chase it out. When it's in, it's in, like a persistent animal friend. Not a pleasant friend, however. More like a friend of the rodent or insect variety. Once in, you can't get it to leave.

In a passably well-heated room, an observant child can stand on a chair and hold her arms above her head, and notice that the air at the top of the room is much warmer than the air on the floor. What is the heat doing up there, anyway? It's useless hovering about the light fixtures and the tops of cupboards. It blows about the spider webs in the corners of the rooms, and ruffles the plastic grocery bags containing long forgotten vacuum cleaner attachments, abandoned on the upper reaches of shelves.

If warm air had an expression, it would be a smirk. If cold air had an expression, it would be a glare. And when cold air pushes into a room, warm air laughs and runs away. *You can't catch me!* Except it can. Cold air will always win. It can push any shred of warm air right out of the room.

Elisabeth squatted in front of the kitchen wood stove, fighting the sub-zero temperatures and an uncooperative draft, as well as damp kindling, trying to light something akin to a fire that might at least warm up the kitchen. Mum was having another one of her days, and Elisabeth needed to figure out the heat situation before running out to her part-time job at the library, where she would shelve books until nine.

Mum could at least have gotten the wood stove going, Elisabeth thought, *instead of letting the house get so cold*. Then she chastised herself inwardly, reminding herself that when Mum wasn't feeling well, it wasn't possible for her to get dressed, never mind coax a fire out of the leaky old kitchen wood stove. And Elisabeth was a champion at getting cold stoves to light. So it probably made sense after all for Elisabeth to be the one to do it, even if it had to wait until after school.

She also had a research paper due tomorrow, as luck would have it. Good thing she worked at the library, where she could grab some books for the paper. She'd be up late tonight. But hey, that was nothing new. Being short of sleep was part of the high school experience.

And there was that good-looking boy, Shawn. He'd actually spoken to her last week. Just to ask her a reference question, but he'd been warm and friendly. Now that they'd spoken, she didn't hesitate to say hello whenever she saw him studying at the library, but she knew that her private fantasies about him were just that, fantasies. He was a nice guy, so he was friendly, but there was no way a guy like him would ever be interested in a girl like her. She'd heard he was going to Harvard next year, whereas she didn't think college could be in the picture for her. There was no money for that, and the thought of school debt made her feel sick inside.

No, she was stuck shelving books at the library for the foreseeable future, at least until something better came along. And that was fine. Well, it wasn't fine, but she could pretend the despair away for a little while longer. As long as she could push away that gnawing sense of being eaten alive inside, she could keep body and soul together.

Elisabeth could hear the fizzing noise of damp wood trying to catch. She leaned forward and blew on the tiny glowing edge of a crumpled edge of newspaper, willing it to flicker its way into the small pile of kindling and sawdust. *Don't go out*, she prayed, but despite her efforts, she saw the orange embers flare brightly for a split second before fading to black. They were out. The sawdust fizzled, then died.

Elisabeth groaned. She reached for the book of matches, then stuck her hand into the stove to rearrange the sticks of wood once more. The ashes were barely warm, and she could feel the icy breeze swirling as she dug around the back of the pile. That was the problem. It was too cold, too windy, and the wood was too wet. Getting an ice-cold stove to light in this kind of weather was going to be a challenge. It never should have been allowed to go out completely, but Mum probably hadn't come downstairs all day long.

I wonder if the barrel in the shed has better sticks, she thought. She didn't think so. It was her job to make sure there was ample kindling and newspaper available, and the boys from down the street had helped her to split logs just a few weeks ago, so she'd already gathered up the chips and bits of scrap lumber from the shed's dirty floor. She thought she'd picked up everything there was to pick up. Not to mention, everything just felt so damp today. There was a new leak in the shed roof, but it was so cold, she didn't think any of the wet had gotten into the woodpile. Most likely, it had frozen itself into the roof corners, providing a weird kind of insulation. A wind break, anyway.

That didn't explain the earlier hissing noise of damp wood in the stove, however. She knew she needed to figure this thing out, or she'd be fighting the same cold stove tomorrow and the day after and the day after. Dear God, couldn't she put this off until tomorrow? She had so many other things to think about today. She could just put on an extra sweater and wear socks to bed.

But she didn't want to leave the house cold, with the wind whipping up the way it was. The radiators had so much trouble pushing heat to the second floor. She knew her mother would be cold, and she didn't want her to lose her temper if by chance she came downstairs and saw that Elisabeth had left for work without getting the kitchen wood stove lit. When Mum really got going, she swirled higher and higher until she crashed. And that wouldn't be a pretty sight to behold. Elisabeth didn't want to have to add her mother's irrational fits to her evening load of homework tonight.

Sighing, Elisabeth stood and threw the book of matches back on the kitchen table. She dusted her hands off on her ash-stained jeans and went to grab her jacket from the coat tree next to the front door. She didn't know how long it would take for her to locate some dry kindling and sticks of wood, so she put on her knit hat and wound her scarf around her neck before digging into her pocket for her work gloves. Thank goodness she never went anywhere without a pair of gloves in her pocket, and these work gloves were sturdy enough to resist the splinters in the woodpile. They were men's gloves, once belonging to her dad.

But she felt reasonably sure that he never wore them for chores, because he'd never done many chores. She almost smiled, but the near-smile triggered a smothered, choked feeling, so instead she pressed her lips together and put on the too-big gloves.

Her dad had been gone now for what felt like a long time, but it had only been two years. She'd been thirteen, and she was fifteen now. It seemed like forever, probably because they'd actually not changed their lives at all since he'd died in that car accident. She still went to school. Mum still hunkered down in the house, reading anything that crossed her path, re-reading things that she'd already read, shuffling about in robe and slippers, screaming at Elisabeth at the top of her lungs when she was having a bad day. Once in a while they went to church, because the church held bean suppers that were cheap and filling. The church ladies, in their tactful Yankee fashion, were solicitous but did not pry. Much.

Dad had died in a fiery explosion of speed and metal. The house was dying quietly in dust and decay. And what about them? Mum in her stained sweatshirt and jeans? Elisabeth in her floral dresses made of old curtains? They were dying, too, although you could say that about all living organisms on the planet. Everyone was dying all the time. And they were dying even before Dad died. Dad wasn't a big one for any kind of work or forward motion. When Mum got crazy and starting shouting because Dad was such a poor provider, Dad would slip out of the house and not return for hours. And at the end of it all, they were just marching toward an inevitable joining with the earth. There was no point to anything, any of the emotion or the effort. *We're all compost*, Elisabeth thought.

Elisabeth picked up the big plastic bucket from next to the wood stove and went through the kitchen to the back door. She pulled it open with difficulty, her gloves slipping round the heavy brass doorknob. It was so windy that the minute she pushed open the storm door, it was snatched out of her hand and slammed wide open with a bone-rattling crash. She reached out, grabbed the cheap metal handle, struggled to pull it closed, but for a moment it seemed the wind would win the battle. She had to use two hands, the bucket swinging wildly in the wind, to get both the door to the house behind her and the storm door in front of her shut, and nearly tumbled down the short staircase into the backyard.

To the rear and left of the house was a carriage house, a sign of the old days when the Burnhams were a wealthy, professional family. Old Judge Burnham had been both a civic leader and a respected member of the judiciary. The carriage house was stuffed to the gills with junk now, and Elisabeth didn't go in there if she could help it. Some people said the furniture in there was valuable, but she didn't even know what that meant. Why would anyone want broken chairs and sofas with the stuffing hanging out?

Next to the carriage house was a small shed, positioned just right for a truck to back up and dump cordwood next to it onto the lawn to prepare for winter. In days long past, Elisabeth's father would call her to come and help him stack the wood neatly in the shed, and she'd enjoyed it, running back and forth between the lawn and the shed, carrying as many sticks as her small arms could handle. As she got older, she'd learned how to split the logs that were too big for the old antique wood stoves, wielding an ax with passable aim, and collecting the wood chips, bark, and branches that flew off the logs for kindling. The boys down the street helped her, and it was sometimes even fun. When her dad died, she discovered that she no longer enjoyed handling the wood in the shed, but she was glad he'd taught her what to do.

If Elisabeth did a good enough job with the stove, maybe she could sit up late in the kitchen with a cup of tea while she did that research paper. But if she couldn't get the stove to stay lit, she would have to work in her bedroom, sitting on the floor with her back against the anemic radiator. She much preferred the popping and crackling of live coals in the wood stove over the hissing and wheezing of the upstairs radiator, so she was going to see if she could make it work.

She had slid the shed door securely shut just the day before, in anticipation of snow squalls, so she tugged hard at the sticky sliding door now until it groaned and yielded to pressure, opening about a foot before it ground to a halt. There was ice and grit and gravel in the track along the top of the sliding door, and she couldn't push it open any further.

Elisabeth slipped into the narrow gap of the doorway, and in response to the wind whipping at her nose and cheeks, tugged desperately at the door until it creaked and slid shut again. All was quiet and pitch-black inside the shed. She moved forward carefully, then felt around with her left hand until she found the light switch. For a moment, she fumbled with her dad's ill-fitting gloves until she got a grip and flipped it.

She gasped.

There was a boy about her age perched on the stack of wood at the far end of the shed. He wore a heavy dun-colored coat and knit cap, and had his knees drawn up under his arms.

He was staring straight at her, an intent expression on his face.

"Shhh," he said. He put his finger to his lips, then nodded at her.

Elisabeth dropped her bucket. It clattered to the ground and rolled briefly before stopping itself with its handle.

Far off, under the yowl of the wind, she could hear someone calling.

"Char-LIEEE!"

It was like a tune, with the first syllable sung low and the second syllable sung high and loud, drawn out for several seconds beyond the first syllable.

"Char-LIEEE!"

Elisabeth stood frozen, not daring to move.

The boy kept his finger on his lips. He bent his head, listening, staring into the distance.

The sound didn't seem to be from outside, where the wind continued to howl. It seemed to come from behind the boy.

2

———

A gust of wind rattled violently at the sliding door, which ran only along a top track and swung free at the bottom. For some reason that Elisabeth had never understood, the placement of the shed was such that the wind never entered as a draft. Instead, it grabbed the thin planks of the walls and shook them hard. Perhaps this was the reason it was built the way it was, behind the carriage house, kitty-corner from the main house, and with that awful sliding door. There was a gap underneath the door, but snow never came in so long as you shut it. The workmen who had built it who knows how long ago had tacked stiff tar paper along the loose bottom edge, and it miraculously was enough to do the job of keeping drafts out, even though it didn't entirely fill the gap. And the top track wasn't smooth, but if you put enough muscle into it, the door would always open or shut.

Elisabeth thought she heard the shouts of more than one voice but couldn't be sure. She listened. No one else called. She bent to pick up the bucket from the ground.

"I'm gonna get a scolding," the boy said. But despite the gloomy words, a bright smile had broken out over his face.

He looked like a brown bird, with his head cocked, listening for more shouts. Elisabeth could see longish chocolate-brown hair combed back over his ears, under his cap, and his eyes were brown. He also had brown smudges on his cheeks, which she suddenly realized was strange, given the wintry landscape outside. The floor of the shed was dirt, however. Maybe he'd been hiding behind the woodpile?

"What are you doing here?" she said, finally. She almost said, "Who are you?" But she knew he was Charlie, of course.

The voices that were calling for him had ceased.

"Hiding."

"I see that. From whom?"

"Everyone."

"Who's everyone?"

Charlie shrugged, but his eyes gleamed, and one corner of his mouth turned up in a mischievous smile.

"Aren't you cold?" Elisabeth asked. But even as the words left her mouth, she knew the answer.

"Cold? Naw. It's fine in here. Out of the wind. And I can hear when people are coming in to get wood. Then I jump in back of —" He pointed to the wall far to his left, at the end of the row. Elisabeth looked. There was a gap between the neatly stacked piles and the wall. Had that been there before? She couldn't remember, which annoyed her, since she had spent hours stacking wood in this shed.

"You're hiding behind the woodpile?"

Charlie beamed. "Yeah. The wood over there is too green to burn. No one goes there. It'll be a while before it's dry enough to use. Maybe a couple years, even."

Elisabeth discovered that she had been holding the kindling bucket in clenched hands. She put it down on the floor in front of her, and Charlie's eyes wandered over to it.

"Whatcha got there?"

"I came to get kindling."

"That's a strange-looking bucket." He frowned, then jumped down easily from his perch. He walked over to where she stood with her back to the sliding door and squatted down to examine the bucket. It was nothing special, just a jumbo-sized plastic bucket with a thin metal handle, the kind you got at the hardware store, filled with paint or some other messy home improvement substance. It was ugly, but serviceable.

"I've never seen anything like this," Charlie went on. He touched the sides of the bucket with both hands. "It's slippery. Is it painted? Or covered with something? It's slick." He rubbed at the bucket more vigorously and seemed fascinated.

Elisabeth didn't know what to say. It was a 5-gallon bucket, white, with the fading blue logo of some paint company stenciled on it.

"It's just plastic," she said.

"What's plastic?"

She wondered if he was pulling her leg, but he looked up at her inquiringly. Before she could think of a reply, he continued, "And where'd you put the lamp you brought?"

"What lamp? I didn't bring a lamp—" She looked at the light switch, and Charlie followed her gaze. He jumped up and headed toward it. Suddenly, the shed went dark.

"What'd I do?" she heard him shout.

"You turned off the light! Turn it back on!"

"I didn't do anything!" he protested, but he sounded spooked, so Elisabeth took pity on him and reached out into the dark with her left hand. At first, her hand brushed the front of Charlie's coat because he was standing beside the light switch, but she managed to reach past him and fumble with the switch.

Light flooded the shed once more.

But the crooked grin had fallen from Charlie's face, and he was looking up at the overhead light fixture with an expression halfway between confusion and amazement. Then he lowered his gaze until he was staring straight at Elisabeth.

"I've never seen that before. Has that always been up there?"

"Uh—" Elisabeth hesitated. She couldn't remember. Had there always been an overhead light? The rooms in the house had no overhead lighting, so why was there a light up there? Would Daddy have put that in? Then she almost chuckled. No, Daddy would not have spent the time or money to put a light in the shed. He didn't come in here pretty much ever. He didn't even split a lot of wood; he let Elisabeth and the boys from down the street do that. That light must have been there from a long time ago.

"I think it's been there for years. Since before I was born, anyway. And probably before my dad was born. Maybe my grandfather put that in."

"When was your dad born?"

It had been a long time since Elisabeth had thought about her dad's birthday, so she had to stop and think for a moment. "Um, let's see. I think 1955. March."

At this, Charlie stared at her. Then he laughed and shook his head. "You mean 1855."

Elisabeth let out a sharp gasp of laughter. "No! Of course not. I don't—that makes no sense. I meant 1955." Charlie frowned. He put his hands on his hips and looked back up at the light fixture above them.

Elisabeth shivered and pulled her coat a little more tightly around her. It was true that the shed had no drafts, but the wind was buffeting the little structure about, and the walls were radiating cold. She glanced at the far wall, where Charlie had been sitting.

"What were you doing in here?" she asked. If his parents were out looking for him, she needed to convince him to leave. It wasn't nice to let your parents think you had run away from home. "Your parents—they must be worried. It's dark, and it's getting colder."

Charlie wasn't listening. He was still looking at the light, his forehead wrinkled. Without altering his stance, he said, "You're just kidding me. About your dad being born in 1955."

Elisabeth bent to pick up the bucket. If he wouldn't leave, then fine. But she needed kindling, she needed to warm up the house, and she needed to get ready for work.

"Maybe it was 1956. I haven't thought about it in a long time. Look, it's weird that you're hiding in our shed, okay? You should go home. I feel bad for whoever is out there looking for you." She began walking toward the rear wall of the shed. "You're right, the wood on that side"—she pointed toward her right—"is still green. I think I screwed up and tried to light a fire with some of it. It's still damp. No wonder it's smoking up the wood stove. I think the stuff you were sitting on is better."

She reached the pile, looked around for the big bin of kindling that was usually next to the wall to her left. "Did you move the trash barrel that was here?"

"What's your name?"

She half-turned, frowning. Charlie was watching her, his arms folded. Something about his posture looked hostile, she thought. He looked to be her age, but she knew all the fifteen-year-olds in Greenleigh. Did he go to private school? There was a parochial school in Greenleigh, but it only went up to eighth grade. If you wanted Catholic high school, you needed to bus into the next big town. And there were prep schools galore all over New England, but those kids had parents who were big shots in Greenleigh, and Elisabeth would have known who they were. She didn't know this kid. Plus, many of the prep school kids started out in Greenleigh public school, and she would have known them and their families that way, too. There shouldn't have been a teenager in Greenleigh whom she'd never met.

"Elisabeth. My name's Elisabeth. I need to get that kindling and go, I don't want to be late for work. But I need that barrel. I can't imagine where it's gone. I'm sure I was the last person in here. Well, except for you." She eyed him suspiciously, but he had left his hostile pose and was pacing a little, looking restless, not paying attention to what she was saying. Could he have taken the barrel of kindling? But why? It was freezing out. He wouldn't have dragged it outside for any reason. And that sliding door—it would have been much too heavy to push wide open while dragging that barrel. And to what purpose? She would have seen it outside if he had pushed it out the door.

She paused, considering. If she had left it outside, it could have toppled over and rolled away in the wind, she supposed. Then she shook her head. It had been full of what Daddy called junk wood, shards of broken wooden things or stuff that was pulled down here and there around the property, even branches and twigs and sawdust. It was heavy. No amount of wind would have knocked it over. And it shouldn't have been outside at all. No one would touch something like that except her.

She looked slowly about her, from one side of the shed to the other. Where could it be? Kicked over onto the floor? Pushed into a dark corner?

Elisabeth noticed a maroon-colored shape lying at the top of the woodpile, half hidden in the shadows where Charlie had been sitting. A book, bound in leather. It had once been sturdy, but now looked old and worn. It looked familiar. There were old books in boxes in the attic, and sometimes she dug through them, marveling at the detritus of people's lives. What had once been important to someone, was now a dusty relic in an attic, unloved and forgotten.

She reached out and picked it up. The words "love poems" were tooled on the front in fading gold letters.

"What's this?" she asked. She started to open it, but her gloves made her hands clumsy.

"Don't touch that," Charlie said sharply. He rushed over and took it from her grasp. "That's my sister's book. I'm not supposed to have it. She's going to be mad if she finds out I brought it out here."

Elisabeth shrugged, nettled. She didn't take kindly to being scolded in her own shed. "Fine. Did you move the big trash barrel? It should have been right here." She pointed. "That's where all the junk wood goes, for kindling."

"Elisabeth, you've got your numbers all mixed up," Charlie said. He'd slipped the book into a pocket. "Your father can't have been born in 1955. It's January 1895. Right now. So you're not making any sense."

Elisabeth burst out laughing. "What are you talking about? It might have been 1956. I could be wrong about 1955. But it's definitely not 1895 now. Are you playing some kind of game? Putting on a play or something? And why are you in our shed?"

Charlie's eyes flashed. "Wait just one minute. Why are you in *our* shed? And I'm not playing a game—well, at least not with you, I'm not. I was just trying to get some time away from the noise in the house, and I didn't want to have to take a bath before driving out to Aunt Sarah's in North Adams. I figured I'd hide out here until it was almost time to go, and then it would be too late for them to make me—well, anyway, never mind that. Why are you taking wood from our shed? Don't you have wood in your own shed? Where do you live, anyway? Are you visiting someone in Greenleigh?"

Elisabeth bristled. "How do you not even know where you are? Or who I am, for that matter? The Burnhams have been in this house since the beginning of time! How can you possibly not know the Burnhams of Greenleigh?"

"Everyone knows the Burnhams," Charlie said in a complaining tone. "But I don't know who *you* are. Are you related to them? Is that why you're in our shed?"

Elisabeth sighed. "This is *our* shed. That's why I'm looking for *our* kindling. Because I have to light *our* wood stove. I don't know what you're doing here, but your parents will be looking for you. And I really need to get kindling." She looked around for odd bits of branches on the floor, but just as she had recalled, the floor had been picked up and was clean. There were a few pine boughs, but those would be green and useless.

Suddenly she stopped, and it was as if the bottom had dropped out of her stomach, like that time Daddy had taken her to the county fair and she'd gone up in the Ferris wheel. It had come sailing down in a curved arc, at a speed she thought had to be too fast, and it felt like she'd left her stomach up at the top even though her body was plummeting downward with the ground rushing toward her face. She turned slowly to Charlie, who was staring at her, his eyes wide.

"Elisabeth Burnham," he whispered.

"North Adams," Elisabeth whispered.

They stared at each other.

This was impossible, Elisabeth thought. Impossible.

But she knew who Charlie was.

Only thing was—he should have been dead.

3

———————

"Are you a ghost?" Elisabeth said, finally.

"You're the ghost," Charlie said. "Are you telling me that—that—"

"My name is Elisabeth Burnham. And I know who you are. You're Charlie Davis." Elisabeth pointed at him with a shaking hand. "That book—I know that book."

Slowly, Charlie took it out of his pocket.

"It says Mary Elisabeth Davis on the front overleaf. Am I right? Elisabeth spelled with an 's.'"

"Yeah. Yeah, that's right. Mary Elisabeth's my sister. Aunt Elisabeth gave her this book."

"I know that book," Elisabeth whispered. "It's poetry. I've read it. Lots of times. And my name is Elisabeth, spelled with an 's.'"

"It's a Burnham thing," Charlie said. "The Burnhams always need to be contrary. Can't spell a name like everyone else does."

"That's exactly what my dad used to say," Elisabeth said. "And I remember North Adams. I haven't been there in forever, but that's where the Moores live. Am I right? You said you were going to see your Aunt Sarah. That's Sarah Moore. And the

Moores are related to the Burnhams somehow. I don't remember how—is Aunt Sarah a Burnham?"

"Naw, Aunt Sarah is a Robertson. She married a Moore. But her sister married a Burnham, and that's why she's everyone's Aunt Sarah. But—are you from the future?" Charlie's voice sank into a whisper.

"God, I don't know. I don't know anything anymore. Including where the stupid kindling barrel is! Maybe that explains it. Maybe in 1895 you didn't have a plastic trash barrel for your kindling."

"I don't know," Charlie confessed. "I don't live here."

"I actually know that," Elisabeth said. "I've seen your name. You live in—"

"Linfield. We're just visiting. Mother and Aunt Elisabeth were friends in school. Best friends. That's why my sister Mary is named Mary Elisabeth. We come here to visit a lot. Every winter and every summer for a few weeks." Charlie looked around. "Am I in your time? Or are you in mine?"

"I'm scared to find out," Elisabeth said.

"Which would be better?"

Elisabeth hesitated. It was terrifying to think that maybe she had been catapulted back into 1895. How would she get back to her own time? Would she get fired from her job? And Mum! Mum! The wood stove! Who would do all the chores that Mum couldn't do?

The panic in her head was like a ping-pong ball, zipping from one problem to the next. Within her heavy gloves, she could feel her palms sweat.

Charlie was saying thoughtfully, "I wouldn't mind living in the future. I kind of like the light up there." He gestured vaguely toward the ceiling. "And I don't like chores. Or working at the mill."

"I need to get back," Elisabeth said. "My mum counts on me

to keep the house going. I have a job at the library, and they'll fire me if I don't show up. And school—I can't just disappear from school."

"So you like your life? Can you tell me about it? What's it like in 1995?" Charlie sounded wistful. "I don't like mine much. Mary Elisabeth got to go away to school. She's got lots of friends, like Mother does. I don't really have friends like that. I don't have any friends at all. Except for the guys at the mill." He kicked at a twiggy branch of pine with his foot, but only succeeded at moving it slightly.

Elisabeth was taking deep breaths, trying to ward off panic. "Don't you go to school?" she said automatically.

"I'm supposed to take over the business from Father," Charlie grumbled. "So I didn't get sent away. Although I would much rather they had sent me. It's so boring to stay in Linfield. And I don't like the sawmill. The men are rough. They drink a lot, and I don't like it."

Elisabeth tried to put her panic on pause for a moment. What sawmill? She tried to think. Sawmills did what—cut logs? Then she had a flash of insight. The logs that ended up as cordwood for the wood stoves for the winter started out as trees. The trees came from a woodlot on the edge of town, from a farm that Daddy used to say was a "connection" of the Burnhams. And those logs went through the Linfield Mill in Linfield. For the longest time she'd thought the Linfield Mill made flour, because she didn't connect the word "mill" with her annual wood-splitting ritual in the fall.

"Sawmill? Your father owns the Linfield Mill?"

"Right outside of Greenleigh," Charlie sighed.

The Linfield Mill still existed in Elisabeth's Greenleigh experience. She had no idea if Charlie's descendants still owned it or operated it. It might have been sold or passed to a cousin or someone not in the Davis family. In fact—

She tried to remember where the Davises had gone. She had once asked Daddy, but she couldn't remember the answer. Daddy had known all the family history and stories dating back to the glory days of the Burnhams, but he was indifferent to it, and never mentioned it unless Elisabeth asked. She had asked repeatedly when she was younger, but as she got older and Daddy absented himself from home more often because of his "sales trips," those opportunities had fallen off.

She shook herself. She couldn't remember what she'd heard about the Davises, but that wasn't important right now. She needed to figure out where she was, and more importantly, *when* she was. Had she zoomed back in time? Was she about to face Greenleigh in 1895?

She needed to get back to Mum. What would Mum do without her?

Although...she had to acknowledge that without Mum, there was no yelling. No rants, no hurried efforts to shut windows so that the entire street didn't hear Mum going off into one of her fits of rage. That would be quite a different life. A life without the constant fetching, carrying, and monitoring of Mum's moods.

Elisabeth tried to steady her trembling hands by clenching them into fists. Charlie apparently noticed.

"Hey Elisabeth. Don't worry. Maybe when you leave the shed, you'll go back into your own time."

"How are you so calm?" Elisabeth retorted.

Charlie blinked, then shrugged. "I dunno. I feel like I know where I am. And—you're practically related to me. I think? Are we cousins? That makes us kin!"

Elisabeth shook her head. "I don't know. We're connected to the Davises somehow, but I don't know exactly how."

"Well, anyway, I'm just not worried. I'm not scared, anyway.

What could happen? I'm still in Greenleigh, and we're still visiting Aunt Elisabeth."

"So wait," Elisabeth said slowly. "You're visiting my—" She paused, wrinkling her forehead. "Your Aunt Elisabeth is my—" She cast an apologetic look at Charlie. "I'm sorry, I think she's my great-great-grandmother. Which must feel strange for you to hear."

"But that makes little sense. Aunt Elisabeth doesn't have children."

"You're right. That makes no sense. But look. I came in here for kindling to light the stove. And I'm worried that I'll be late for work. Except maybe I'm not in my time anymore. When I go back into the house, I'm either going to find your Aunt Elisabeth, or you're the one who isn't where he's supposed to be."

"Well, of course I'm not where I'm supposed to be," Charlie retorted. "I was hiding here in the woodshed. I've been here all afternoon."

"Either that, or you're a ghost, or I'm a ghost." Elisabeth paused, then added, "I don't believe in ghosts."

"Can I go into the house with you?" Charlie asked. His eyes sparkled. "I want to know who's in there. This is exciting!"

"There's a chance you'll get punished for hiding in the woodshed when you should've been doing chores," Elisabeth said severely.

"All right. I'm ready for that, if you're ready to deal with my Aunt Elisabeth. And my mother. That'll be a lot of fun to watch —a girl from the future, and my mother! I wonder what she'll say?" Charlie sounded gleeful. Then he sobered. "What about your mother? What will she do if she sees me?"

Elisabeth was walking back toward the shed door. "Nothing," she said over her shoulder.

"Nothing?" Charlie followed, giving the light switch another curious glance.

"Nothing," Elisabeth said shortly. "She's not well and spends most of the day upstairs. If you're the one who's visiting my time, you could spend years in my house and she'd never know you were there. If that's what you want, of course." She paused, her hand on the sliding door. "After we figure this out, Charlie, we'll have a different problem. We'll need to think about how to get us back into the right times."

"I don't know if I want to go back to my time," Charlie said.

"Well, you can't stay in mine," Elisabeth retorted. "Where will you go? Where will you live?"

"I'm your cousin," Charlie said, grinning. "We're kin. And your mother doesn't have to know I'm in the house. You said so yourself."

Elisabeth nearly groaned. This kid! None of this was amusing, but he was having fun at Elisabeth's expense. He truly wasn't upset at the idea that he might be trapped a hundred years in the future. He seemed to think this inadvertent time travel was a game. And if it were she who was trapped in 1895, that, too, did not seem to perturb him.

What would she do if she were stuck in 1895? Putting Mum aside for a moment—what would that even be like?

It might not be bad, she admitted to herself. If indeed "kin" was what mattered, perhaps the Burnhams would accept her, because she was a Burnham. Imagine that, being "enough" because you were born just the way you were, with your name and identity exactly what it was.

She'd never explored a connection with the Burnhams before. Mum loathed anything and everything related to the Burnhams. She was furious that Daddy had never held a decent job, had squandered his modest Burnham trust fund, and had no desire to do anything or be anything beyond who and what he was, a Burnham of Greenleigh.

Maybe living as a Burnham in 1895 Greenleigh was a way out of her sad life in 1995 Greenleigh?

No, what was she thinking?

Frustrated, Elisabeth tugged at the sliding door. She couldn't have such an absurd argument with a ghost from the past! If he was a ghost, that is. Perhaps Elisabeth herself was the ghost. In any case, she couldn't leave Charlie in the shed, not in temperatures that would surely plummet to single digits overnight. She needed to find out who or what was in the house and then go from there.

4

———

"There's a trick to that door," Charlie said, coming up behind her.

"I know what the trick is, you need to—"

"Lift it up," Charlie finished, and together they lifted and pulled. The door glided smoothly, and they stepped out. For a moment, they stood still, braced against the wind, peering around the yard. As far as Elisabeth could tell, nothing had changed. The wind still blew, and the carriage house sat quietly in the late afternoon winter dark. No lights were on in the main house. That could mean that she was safely in her own time, with Mum still upstairs in her room. Or it could mean that Charlie's sister and mother had left for North Adams on their visit to Aunt Sarah. Nothing looked out of the ordinary to Elisabeth, but then, nothing about this view had changed in the past two hundred years, most likely.

Charles had already tugged the shed door shut behind them. She could sense his eagerness as he stood behind her, impatiently waiting for her to lead the way. *Why are teenaged boys so rash*, she thought, irritated. *Why isn't he worried or upset?* Surely the life he led was not so awful that he was eager to leave everyone and everything he knew. Although she conceded a point, which was that in a way, he wasn't a stranger at all. He seemed to know her house and Greenleigh as well as she did. He might feel just fine in the Greenleigh of 1995.

She, on the other hand, thought about turning over a new leaf—becoming someone else, somewhere else—and her heart gave an odd little flutter in her chest. She had never felt this way before, had never considered, even for a second, the possibility that life elsewhere could even exist for her. Linfield? North Adams? Or even here in Greenleigh, or even here in this very house—but not now, and not with Mum.

A sudden rush of guilt came over her. But at the same time, her heart protested, with the memory of Mum shouting at Daddy that she would have left him long ago but for "his" daughter. For she looked nothing like Mum, who had striking dark eyes and hair. Elisabeth was a mousy, skinny thing with plain brown hair and eyes, looking exactly as mousy and boring as all the Burnham relatives in their stern portrait poses. When she was little and would forget to show up for dinner because she was daydreaming, Mum would throw her hands up in exasperation and declare, "You're just like your father." Because she *was* like her father.

If not for Elisabeth, Mum would have gone back to Vermont, back to the people she knew. She would have gotten the heck out of Greenleigh, where everyone knew everyone's business, and where she had to make do with a giant mansion that shook and rattled with every gust of wind, a house that wouldn't heat in winter and wouldn't cool in summer, a house that was falling down around her faster than she could fix it with her meager skills. Back in Vermont, she'd been an actress, a fixture in the local community theater scene. She could sing, dance, and play the piano. She used to teach piano lessons and had a good side gig as a wedding organist. There were things she could do, people she could reach out to.

Leaving Mum might make her happy. Mum could get the heck out of Greenleigh and forget that this chapter of her life had ever happened. She'd be able to rid herself of Elisabeth and the heavy weight of the Burnham history, all those boxes and old furniture in the attic. She could sell the old Burnham manse and return to her maiden name and lead a different life, one that wasn't filled with disappointment and broken promises. Maybe she could go to Boston or New York. Maybe she could start over, even in her forties. It was possible, if she didn't have to think about a kid and the only asset her worthless husband had left behind.

It occurred to Elisabeth that Charlie had said little about the life he led in Linfield. Maybe there was something there he was happy to ditch. He'd mentioned not wanting to take over the family business, but given that the sawmill was operating well into the twentieth century and nearly the twenty-first, Elisabeth doubted that he knew any kind of privation. His sister had gone to a fancy school, so the family was clearly willing to spend money on education. It was a pity that Charlie wasn't keen on taking over the sawmill, but he'd eventually be a wealthy gentleman with property. That couldn't be so bad.

I'd do it in a heartbeat, Elisabeth thought. Imagine that, a steady income. No financial worries. And not only that—a place where one belonged.

Sure, she belonged here at the house on Church Street. But it wasn't anything she had earned or worked for. It was just an old house. A sad mother and sad memories. Not the way to move forward in life. Charlie, on the other hand, could be a contributor. Someone who did things. Not like her.

She turned to Charlie. "All right, then. Let's go," she said, her voice muffled by her scarf. She raised her voice when she saw that Charlie had to lean in to hear her above the wind. "If your mother and sister are there, you must hide me somehow. Unless you think they won't mind a visitor from the future."

"They're not home," Charlie said. "If they were home, you'd see the buggy out there. And Aunt Elisabeth is with them. But there's a housekeeper and a cook and a gardener and a maid and—"

"Oh, for Pete's sake," Elisabeth said irritably. She turned around and started trudging toward the house. She knew the Burnhams had once been wealthy, but hearing about it in such proximity felt awful, given the depths to which they had fallen. Most of the rooms in the house were shut and falling apart in disuse. Daddy had never been handy, so he didn't care to fix anything. There'd never been money for that, anyway. There was a trust fund that had dripped out all its principal as Daddy tried first one job, then another. He was born to be rich, not to earn a living, Mum had said many times.

She suddenly felt self-conscious about Charlie seeing what the Burnhams had come to. Maybe it really would be better to find herself in Charlie's time instead. As long as Charlie could find some adequate explanation for her presence.

No. No, that wasn't true. It wouldn't be better for her to be stuck in Charlie's time. She needed to be home. Mum needed her. She would not abandon her, even if in theory Mum might be happier without her. Mum wasn't in any shape to take care of herself.

But she could imagine it, almost taste it. Freedom. A different life.

She could imagine herself into one of the old photo albums in the attic, her hair piled atop her head, wearing a long, ruffled skirt. She'd like that, she thought. And back in those days, the house had been in such good shape. It was a beautiful home, and well cared for, it would be a place of pride. Everyone knew the Burnham manse in Greenleigh.

No, this was wrong. She didn't want to walk into 1895 Greenleigh. That would be terrifying. And Mum needed her. No, wait. Mum would be better off without her. No, she wasn't in shape to be on her own. No, she—

She halted. Charlie, who'd been following, ran into her. He was taller than she was, but with a compact and muscular frame, and the weight of his body smacking into her caused her to stumble and nearly fall.

"Hey!" Charlie protested. "I nearly fell over. Nearly knocked you over, too. Why are you stopping?"

Elisabeth shook her head. She had no words for this strange feeling. She was neither here nor there. She was both here *and* there. How was it she was two things at once? She couldn't go back in time. She needed to stay in the life she had. She wanted it to be twentieth century America when she stepped into the house. But what was she stepping into, exactly?

A cold wood stove that wouldn't light. A nearly empty fridge. Latches that didn't work, doors that didn't shut, windows with cracks stuffed with rags. Mouse holes. Midnight squirrel parties in the attic above.

Her backpack full of meaningless textbooks. The rejection letter from the National Honor Society because of that one B-minus in geometry. The sign-up sheet for the driver's education course that she couldn't afford to take. The two-year-old pair of glasses that were now too weak, that she hadn't figured out how to replace.

"Oh, honey," her mother had said, looking blankly at her when she'd tried to show her that the earpieces were starting to detach from the frame. "Daddy had a tiny screwdriver kit for that."

Elisabeth knew about the tiny screwdriver kit but had no

idea where it was. Maybe in the glove compartment of the car that had self-destructed around him in the accident.

She did without the glasses and squinted her way through geometry. It would have helped her grades if she could have seen the board.

The fact was, she didn't know if she wanted to go home, back to 1995. She didn't know if she wanted her life back. It just didn't feel like much of a life.

But what was fair for a girl to expect?

She thought back to the days before Daddy had left and not come home again. Did she want those days, even? Those days when he'd taken to the road for days at a time, and spent the proceeds of his sales trips in the back room of the Athena diner, treating his friends and glad-handing the kitchen staff, leaving big tips and ordering everyone another round of raki?

She felt a horrid, sick pit in her stomach. But what kind of monster was she to want to leave home? The best home that her parents could give her? A home so rooted in their family, that—

"Hey, it's cold," Charlie whined. "Come on!"

Charlie felt no such indecision, apparently. *What a brat.*

Despite the scarf covering her mouth, Elisabeth let out a giggle.

"What is it?" Charlie demanded.

"You wouldn't understand," she said.

"You're making me stand here in the wind! You'd better tell me what's so funny!" Charlie reached out and yanked her scarf down. "All right. What is it? Now I can hear you."

"I don't know," Elisabeth said, "but I don't know if I want to go back to my time. I might well want to be in yours instead."

Charlie squinted in disbelief, then shook his head. He pulled her scarf up again and started trudging toward the house. He said over his shoulder, "You don't know what you're talking about. If you won't go, I'm going."

"Wait," Elisabeth called, panicking. She hurried after him. "Wait. You're headed for the front door. You can't just charge in there."

"Neither can you. Let's creep onto the porch."

"Is there anyone on the street?" Elisabeth said nervously.

Charlie slowed his pace. He looked first in one direction, then another. He shook his head.

"Nope. But I'll tell you what. We don't have those." He pointed at the electric wires leading from the street to the house.

His voice sounded triumphant.

They were not in 1895 Greenleigh after all.

5

———

Elisabeth stopped. "That's it, then," she said. She felt a sharp pang of disappointment. So all the angst-ridden self-torment was for nothing. She would not be leaving her life here in the twentieth century. She'd be able to take care of Mum. She could keep her library job. She could turn in that paper tomorrow. Everything was as usual.

On the street in front of the house she could see dark shapes. Parked cars. She wondered what Charlie would think of automobiles.

Well, she'd have to take the lead, since this was her century.

"You'll be all right with me," she said, walking past him and up the front stairs. "Mum won't have come downstairs. Come into the house out of the cold so we can figure this thing out."

"You said you were going to be late for something," Charlie said, following close behind.

Elisabeth nodded. "You'll have to come with me to work. I work at the library, so it's quiet and we'll have a few hours to think. It won't be strange for you to be there. But come in and help me out with that wood stove."

Charles rubbed his hands together. "Sure thing. I'm a pro."

Elisabeth pulled the storm door open. "I somehow suspected you were," she said dryly.

Charlie seemed fascinated by the front porch. He walked from one end to the other, rubbing his hand on the railing and inspecting the woodwork.

"This is new," he said to Elisabeth as she waited for him to finish his examination, one hand on the door.

"I suppose," Elisabeth conceded. She remembered old black-and-white photos from the thirties, carefully preserved in a leather-bound album on a shelf in the attic. There hadn't been a front porch then. The workmanship wasn't as good as that of the rest of the house, and her father had always complained that he wanted to pull the whole thing down. It was rickety, and he said it was going to introduce rot into the wood where the porch was attached to the main house. There was a growth of gnarled vines over one corner, and no matter how cold it got or how rough the winter was, that vine would not die. Elisabeth had tried to pull it out at one point, but no. It was there to stay. She suspected it had been there long before the porch was built, and that the porch served as a welcome step stool up into the area where people lived.

Funny to think of nature trying to get into the world of people.

For a moment, she stood still, her hand on the door. Then she shook herself. She needed to open the door into the house. She knew she was hesitating because she was afraid. Of what, she didn't know. There was no danger of Mum emerging from her room until it was dinnertime.

Maybe there was some part of her that still hoped, still wondered if she would find a different world in there.

"Let's go in," she said to Charlie, who had returned from his explorations.

She pushed the door open.

It was definitely the twentieth century. The house was just as dark as when she had left it, but it absolutely smelled like home, like old furniture and the smoking old wood stove.

She could feel Charlie right behind her, his breath in her ear as he eagerly anticipated this alternative world.

"Beth? Is that you?"

Mum's voice, calling from upstairs.

"Oh, shoot," Elisabeth breathed. They should have come in the back door. She'd been so intent on checking the street and the front of the house to figure out what century they were in, it hadn't occurred to her that her mother would find it odd to hear the front door open.

"Yeah, it's me," she called. Cautiously, she shut the door behind her. Charlie had already tried to bolt for the front room, but she'd stopped him, pulling him back by the collar of his thick wool coat. She made furious gestures with her hands toward the kitchen, and he looked annoyed, but followed as she walked past the staircase.

"I just got the mail," she added, directing her voice up the stairs. She hoped it was a passable lie. There was no further comment, so she continued toward the kitchen, Charlie practically treading on her heels.

Elisabeth set down her empty bucket and whispered, "Could you get the stove going? Quietly, mind you? Preferably in silence? I need to grab my things from the front room and then we both have to go to the library."

Charlie went over to the wood stove and stood for a moment, peering at it. "This is new," he mouthed at her.

Elisabeth caught herself before she made a sarcastic retort. The stove was far from new. Obviously, it was a good thing that it wasn't the wood stove that Charlie remembered from the 1800s, but this didn't do much to make her feel better.

"Just do it quietly!" she repeated, before heading back out of the kitchen. She went into the front room to grab her school bag, then checked her appearance in the front hall mirror.

She didn't know whom she was kidding—she didn't have to worry about looking good, she thought. She'd be shelving books for a couple of hours, and then she'd be searching frantically for books for that research paper. She didn't even remember what it was on, but she figured she'd just grab whatever books her more responsible classmates hadn't already nabbed and write about whatever topic they hadn't already chosen.

And what was the point of looking good for Shawn Waterstone? That was a lost cause, for sure. If she saw him tonight, she would wave, he would wave, and that would be it. With Charlie in tow, she couldn't even start a conversation, could she?

Unless there were books about witchcraft or time travel in the library, there wasn't anything she could do about Charlie tonight. Where was she going to put him? Would he stay quiet enough not to trigger an unwelcome encounter with Mum?

"Hey," said a voice in her ear, and she spun around to find Charlie grinning at her.

Elisabeth put her finger to her lips and glared at him.

"That's the same mirror as Aunt Elisabeth's," he mouthed.

Elisabeth turned around again, curious in spite of herself. Charlie appeared behind her right shoulder in the mirror, grinning his impish smile.

"It's fancy," he said. "Everything here is so fancy. I love it here. I always have."

Elisabeth almost laughed. What an irony! She and her mother were barely holding everything together, but for Charlie, this house was "fancy."

"Did you get it lit?" she whispered.

"Sure. Easy. It's a great stove. Real tight."

She frowned. It wasn't a great stove, and she had struggled like crazy earlier this afternoon. She didn't believe him.

But indeed he had gotten the stove started. The fire was blazing, the damper only slightly open, showing that he had not only started it, but it had caught beautifully. The kitchen was warm now.

"What d'you use?" she asked suspiciously. Maybe he'd thrown in something that shouldn't have gone in there, like styrofoam or plastic from the trash bin in the far corner. She sniffed the air cautiously but did not detect any fumes.

Charlie pointed. "There's kindling over there. In that basket."

"That stuff is green. I couldn't make it light earlier."

"It's fine." Charlie looked up at the overhead light, which flickered dimly. "You have so many magical things, you've forgotten how to light a stove."

"What?" Elisabeth said hotly. How dare he! She knew how to light a stove, thanks very much! Holding her irritation in check, she decided it wasn't worth the argument. "Come on, we need to get moving." They went back into the front hall, where Elisabeth called up the stairs softly, "Mum? I'm leaving for the library."

There was the sound of a door creaking open. "Beth?"

"Mum?" Elisabeth shot Charlie a dismayed look and waved him into the parlor. Obediently, he slipped into the next room. She started up the stairs.

"I'm leaving for the library," she said.

"I'm cold, Beth."

"I know, Mum. It's nasty outside. Windy." Elisabeth trudged up the stairs. Her mother's bedroom was on the right, next to her own. The door was ajar, so she pushed it open further. Her mother was standing next to the room's radiator, wrapped in a faded pink robe, her arms folded tightly as if to ward off the wind howling outside. She'd brushed her hair today, Elisabeth noticed with relief. She almost looked normal, if normal people typically wore nightgowns all day long.

"I don't know how to get the heat on," her mother said, her voice sounding plaintive.

"The heat's on. I checked," Elisabeth lied. The thermostat for the ancient heating system was on the wall at the top of the stairs, and she hadn't looked at it, but she knew what it would say. She always turned it up high when she got home from school, and it always made little to no difference.

"The radiator's cold."

Elisabeth walked over and put her hand on the radiator. It was faintly warm. If the boiler were on the blink, the painted metal would have been mind-numbingly cold. So this meant that the heat was functional. It was just anemic.

"I'll check the boiler before I leave. Maybe I need to press the red reset button again."

"Can't you get someone in to look at it?" Her mother pulled her robe more tightly around her.

"Why I don't get you a heavier robe, Mum?" Elisabeth went to the huge wooden wardrobe and reached out to pull open a door, but her mother rushed over and pushed her aside.

"What are you doing?" she demanded, her voice rising.

"I'm—I'm—" Elisabeth stammered, but her mother began to shout.

"Don't get into my things, dammit! Keep out of there!"

"All right, all right," Elisabeth said, backing away. "I just thought—"

"Leave my things alone! They're all I've got, and I don't want you to touch them! They're mine!"

"All right," Elisabeth repeated, trying to keep her voice even. She wondered if Charlie could hear them. He probably could, right through the floor register. He was in the room right under them, after all.

"Why do I have to put up with all of this?" Her mother now spoke quietly.

"I'm sorry, Mum. It's cold today. Have you eaten?" Elisabeth ignored the question. It was one that her mother voiced repeatedly. There was no answer, really.

Her mother shook her head. "I'm not hungry."

"I'll go get you something."

"No. Don't."

"Well, there's spaghetti in the fridge from last night. You can have that for dinner."

Her mother nodded.

If this were any other family, now would be a good time for a hug. But this was a taciturn Yankee family, so hugs were not forthcoming.

I could use a hug, Elisabeth thought to herself.

"I'm going, then. I'll be back late, because I have a paper to write. I have to grab some books from the library after I'm done working."

"I'll save you some dinner."

"Don't worry about me. I'm all set. Really."

Elisabeth headed toward the door.

"Beth."

Elisabeth stopped. She turned.

"I'm sorry," her mother murmured. "I know I should do more."

Elisabeth forced a smile. "That's silly. I'm fine. And so are you. See you soon."

But when she got downstairs, Charlie was nowhere to be seen.

6

———

Oh, no.

Elisabeth checked the kitchen, the parlor, and the front room. Not there. Panicking, she ran down the cellar steps. The boiler was roaring its frustrated roar, perhaps furious at its inability to put out heat that would reach the second floor of the house. She couldn't imagine that Charlie would want to be anywhere near it. She took a quick glance around in the dark, but he surely wouldn't have thought to go into the cellar. And anyway, in the glory days of the Burnhams, only the housekeeping staff would have gone down those steps. It was likely Charlie didn't even know where the cellar door was.

Once more in the kitchen, she went to the back door to look out the window in the shed's direction. Perhaps he went back out to the shed? Maybe he had thought better of that hare-brained scheme of his to stay in the twentieth century. Maybe he had gone back to 1895.

"Beth!"

She jumped and turned. Charlie was standing behind her.

"Charlie!" she exclaimed. "Where were you?"

"Just looking around," he said.

"Looking around where?" Elisabeth squinted suspiciously. "I looked in all the rooms down here. I thought maybe you'd gone back to the shed."

Charlie laughed. "I wouldn't do that! Why would I go out into the cold? I'm going to stay right here in this house, so I figured I'd look around. I was in the attic."

Elisabeth blanched. The attic? He'd gone up into the attic while she was in Mum's room?

"Charlie! You shouldn't have done that! What if Mum had seen you?"

Charlie shrugged. "Then you would have told her I'm just a friend."

"A friend in the attic? I don't think so! Listen, Mum's not stupid. She would have known something was up if she had seen you. And then what?"

"I was quiet!"

"But you walked right past her room! That was dumb!"

"Sorry. I just thought maybe I could live in your attic."

"In our *attic*?"

"Mary Elisabeth and I spent hours up there. It used to be real nice. Rugs and old chairs and stuff. Old books. Toys." Charlie's voice trailed off. For a moment, he looked as if he were daydreaming.

"Huh. Well, I'll bet today it looked different," Elisabeth said shortly. The attic! It was a dump. Cobwebs and broken furniture. Boxes and boxes of books that were wormy and falling apart. It smelled like old stuff.

"It did." Charlie's eyes came back into focus, and he looked stern. "Why is it such a mess?"

Elisabeth sighed. "Come on, Charlie. I need to get to the library. Let's go. You'll have to come with me."

She picked up her bag from where she had dumped it

earlier. She placed a finger on her lips and gave Charlie a warning look before calling up the stairs, "Bye, Mum."

There was no reply, so they let themselves out the door.

Once on the street, Elisabeth quickened her pace. Her mind kept turning over the problem of Charlie. What to do about him? In theory, he could stay in the house as long as he kept out of Mum's way. She couldn't take him to school and he couldn't walk around Greenleigh during school hours or the truant officers would catch him. But until she figured out how to get him back home, in theory he could stay.

"How old are you, Charlie?" The gusty wind had settled into a stiff breeze, so she leaned into it as she trudged, pulling the scarf slightly away from her mouth to speak.

"Seventeen," he replied.

"No! I thought you were younger."

Charlie lifted his shoulders, shrugged. He was looking around Church Street, his eyes wide, taking in the occasional parked car, peering up at the traffic lights as Elisabeth tugged his elbow to stop him from walking through an intersection without stopping.

"That's a red light. You can't go through a red light."

"But that person over there is," he said, pointing.

"I know, people do that sometimes. It's called jaywalking, and it's dangerous. Don't do it. Sometimes the cars go fast and you could get hurt."

"So no more horses in the twentieth century," Charlie said, staring with fascination as a string of slow-moving vehicles rolled by.

"Not unless you live on a farm or something," Elisabeth said. "Charlie, you don't go to school?"

"Nope. I work at the mill. I wish I went to school. I hate the mill."

"But your father owns it."

They started walking again as the light above turned green, and an expression of understanding crossed Charlie's face.

"I understand now. Red for stop, green for go. I wish I could have kept going to school. It's not like we can't afford it."

"Was there something you wanted to study?"

Charlie ducked his head, looking a little embarrassed. He patted his pocket, where he had stashed Mary's poetry book earlier.

"I want to write."

"Write?" Elisabeth raised her voice. She wasn't sure she'd heard him correctly.

Charlie patted his right-hand pocket again. "I read all of Mary Elisabeth's books. She has so many, she hardly notices. She gets them at school. And Father buys them for her all the time. And Aunt Elisabeth, too. I have to sneak around to read them. But I always take one to the mill with me when I go in. Sometimes I can spend an entire afternoon reading, if no one catches me."

"But how do you do that? Don't you get into trouble?" The thought of disappearing for an entire afternoon! Elisabeth wondered if anyone would notice if she didn't show up for any of her afternoon classes at school. Well, it wouldn't make a difference, because obviously Mum would notice if she didn't come home. There would be no heat and nothing for dinner. So skipping school didn't amount to much in the way of freedom. Home was the problem, not school.

She wondered if this was why Charlie was so unconcerned about being stuck in the twentieth century and absent from his own. Did no one in his family care that he was missing?

"Sometimes," Charlie was saying in an off-hand manner, "Aunt Elisabeth asks me about poetry, and we talk about it." He ducked his head, a little embarrassed. "She has so many poetry books. She knows so much."

Poetry, thought Elisabeth in amazement. So the men of the family worked, and the ladies were sent to school? Was this how it had always been in the extended Burnham clan? No wonder Daddy was miserable. He would much rather have avoided work and read poetry instead.

Things were different in the twentieth century, she mused. Education was to get you that good job. Daddy had gone to a small college in Vermont. Lots of Burnhams had gone there. And he met Mum there. Her family was an old New England family, too. Sometimes she'd taught piano lessons before Daddy's accident. She could sing, cook, embroider...she could do all the things that Charlie's female relatives were probably taught to do in school.

But Daddy had done nothing with that fine liberal arts education. He'd wanted to become a musician, then a writer, then a painter. The scattered debris of his ambition lay all over the attic. Sometimes Elisabeth wished she could throw it all away. She knew it was painful for Mum to think about how miserable Daddy had been, trying to scrape a living together out of too much education and not enough backbone. Or at least, that's what Mum had called it.

Elisabeth looked at Charlie, who was peering into the shop windows of the principal shopping street of Greenleigh with fascination. What a strange alignment and yet misalignment, she thought. We're alike and yet not alike.

"Beth!" At first, she thought it was just the ringing in her ears from the wind, which had slackened somewhat but was still blowing stiffly. But she felt Charlie's pace slow down behind her, so she turned and saw old Mrs. Miller hurrying toward them.

"I was at the ATM when I saw you. How's your mum?"

"Fine, thank you," Elisabeth said automatically, raising her voice as Mrs. Miller put a hand behind her ear and leaned forward to listen. "Everything's fine."

"Good, good. Glad to hear it." Mrs. Miller, a sprightly older woman in her sixties, sported a black acrylic yarn hat and matching gloves that were pilled and had seen better days. Her long down coat looked warm but was leaking feathers from the seams. She looked Charlie up and down, peering through silver bifocals perched on the edge of her nose.

"This is Charlie," Elisabeth said. She also turned to give Charlie an assessing glance, hoping that nothing screamed "nineteenth century" about his attire. His coat was made of good-quality wool in an earthy shade of brown. Perhaps it was unusual for a teenaged boy to even bother with a hat and gloves, but when the temps were in the teens or below, even the hardiest Greenleigh boys bundled up. His shoes were good leather boots, which might be a little odd in an era when boys wore athletic shoes in all seasons of the year, but perhaps Mrs. Miller didn't know what teenaged boys wore on their feet. At least, Elisabeth hoped she didn't.

Charlie stuck out his hand. "Charlie Davis, ma'am."

Mrs. Miller looked taken aback as she shook hands. "Oh!" She turned to Elisabeth. "I didn't know you had family here."

Elisabeth privately cursed. Why did Charlie have to go and say his last name? Of course Mrs. Miller would know that the Burnhams and the Davises were related. She knew everything there was to know about the old families in town. But she was a terrible gossip, and she also had no patience for Mum's mental state. If she wanted to march right over to the house and up the stairs into Mum's room, just to demand answers, she would.

Charlie was beaming. He apparently really enjoyed the idea that he now belonged in twentieth-century Greenleigh.

"Yes, he's just here for a few days. Visiting."

"Well!" Elisabeth imagined that she could see the wheels turning in Mrs. Miller's head. "That's very nice. Which branch of Davises are you from, Charlie?"

"Vermont," Elisabeth said, just as Charlie said, "Linfield."

Mrs. Miller looked from one to the other. "Which is it?" she demanded.

Charlie looked at Elisabeth, grinning. "Both," she said. *Darn him!* She wished she could reach out and pinch him, warn him to stay quiet. "His folks have a place in Vermont and a place in Linfield."

"That's very interesting," Mrs. Miller said. "You might know the Beaseleys? They're in Linfield. Very good friends of my late husband."

"I sure do—" Charlie began, but Elisabeth jumped in, eager to prevent more opportunities for slip-ups.

"Mrs. Miller, I'm freezing! You must be freezing, too. I'm going to be late for work, I'm so sorry—"

"No, no. You're right, it's too cold to stand around talking. Well, it's very nice meeting you, Charlie. How long are you staying?"

"Just for a few days," Elisabeth interrupted before Charlie could reply. "Have a good evening, Mrs. Miller!"

"See you on Sunday, Beth." Mrs. Miller gave her a quick nod, but as Elisabeth turned to continue her way down the street, she could sense her curious gaze.

"What's the A-T-M? Some kind of Ladies' Aid Society thing?" Charlie asked cheerfully.

"Don't say your full name when people ask you," Elisabeth hissed under her breath. "The old ladies at church know we're related to the Davises. Other people might know, too."

"Isn't that a good thing? I fit in here. I'm part of the family. It isn't strange that I'm here. Isn't that better?"

"I suppose," Elisabeth conceded. "But not if Mrs. Miller asks my mum about you. Then we have a problem. And anyway, you're not staying here."

"So what's wrong with your mum?" Charlie attempted to change the subject.

Elisabeth ignored the question, hoping that he'd forget he'd asked. They turned a corner. The library was two blocks ahead, a large, ugly fifties-era building in a perfect rectangular block shape.

"That's the library. Please don't talk to the librarians! Just sit at a table and read or something. When I've got my cart set up you can come over to where I'm shelving books and we'll try to figure this thing out."

"I don't want to figure anything out," Charlie objected. "I like it here. And if I'm part of your family, people will accept me. I'll get a job, I won't be a bother."

"Charlie, if you're just going to get a job here, aren't you better off inheriting your dad's mill? Going to school is expensive. Are you sure you'll be able to live a different life? And won't you miss your parents? Your sister?"

"Nope," Charlie said airily. "And you're my family, right?"

"Yes—no—not really," Elisabeth groaned in frustration.

What if she could leave everything behind? Would she? What if she knew she was going to live in the same Greenleigh, with people who were actually her relatives—would she consider going there? Staying there?

I can't leave Mum, she thought. *I just can't.*

And that was that. But a little pit of regret lay in her stomach.

What if she could change everything?

And why did she keep fantasizing about it?

They headed into the library. Elisabeth warned Charlie again not to talk to anyone and pointed him in the direction of the history section. She had to pick up some research books for her American history paper and she would end up there, eventually. She would do her shelving and try to figure out how to get Charlie back to Linfield—in his own time—and after that she'd worry about the stupid paper.

Charlie happily obeyed, although not until he had stood for a full five minutes at the water fountain, marveling at the splashing water, until Elisabeth caught him and marched him away. She made her apologies to the librarians on the evening shift, since she was a few minutes late, and found her cart of books waiting to be shelved.

The smells of floor polish and old books always comforted

her. It smelled like childhood. It had never occurred to her she had spent so many hours here with her father when she was little because he was mostly unemployed. Those had been happy years, in her mind, and they were inextricably tied to the smells and sounds of the children's section at the library. She remembered that he borrowed cassette tapes and vinyl records of the old big band sounds his father had loved, a grandfather she only dimly remembered. They had a fifties-vintage record player in the parlor, and he'd blast the sounds of Glen Miller so loudly that her mother would protest.

She didn't listen to much music anymore, she thought. When had that stopped? Possibly when Daddy had died.

She picked up the next book, but her mind continued to wander as she tried to remember which author name came first, MacDonaldson or McDonald.

Was Charlie going to stay in Greenleigh forever? Could he possibly live in the house with Mum never finding out?

That was a silly question, she thought. Mum would never find out. There were any number of empty rooms. It was unlikely that Mum would ever go into any of them. Charlie could go up and down the back stairs as long as he made sure Mum was nowhere near the kitchen. It was an enormous house.

Mrs. Miller, the church ladies, and Mrs. McPherson next door—they were more problematic. Mrs. Miller had an unending supply of curiosity. She would poke her nose into every nook and cranny if she thought something was fishy. And Mrs. McPherson didn't leave her home much nowadays, because of age and arthritis. She spent a lot of time gardening and peering out the window with her cat. She would catch sight of Charlie eventually, for sure.

And Mrs. Miller had already met Charlie, so she would be sure to ask Elisabeth about her the next time they met. She'd probably ask Mum on Sunday at church, too.

Elisabeth leaned for a moment against the cool books on the shelf directly in front of her. Her head hurt. She hadn't grabbed a snack before leaving the house. She was hungry, she still had a paper due, and now she had Charlie to worry about.

How could Charlie be both here and in her family tree, anyway? How did that work?

She tried to remember if there were any photos of Charlie in the old albums. Now, that would be creepy. She tried to count backwards. If he was a teenager in the 1890s, how old would he have been when the old photos were taken?

If she went back to look at them, what would she find? How could he be both there and here? Then and now?

Then she had another horrid thought. Was *she* in those photos? How did she know if she really belonged in Greenleigh, in the twentieth century? Maybe she didn't belong here at all. Maybe that explained this strange sense of ennui, this weird feeling that she was an intruder in her own home, an unwanted and unexpected being in her own family.

She was tempted to ask Charlie. Did he remember her from his own world? He would have remembered her name, if it had been the same. Maybe she had a different name back then.

She was going insane.

She jerked her head back from the shelf in surprise when she felt a hand on her elbow. An apology sprang to her lips, but the person next to her wasn't a stern librarian.

It was Shawn Waterstone.

She looked up at him blankly. She'd been so careful to mask her expression around him, so careful to always put on that neutral, pleasant expression. Otherwise she thought she might look needy, or desperate, or lonely. But at the moment she was taken by surprise, and given that he was quite a bit taller than her, she stared up at him in a daze, not knowing how she looked.

She must have looked different, because he had been about

to say something, but stopped and looked concerned. "Beth," he began, then paused, his gray-green eyes searching hers.

"Are you all right?"

"Uh—yes. Yes, I'm fine." She tried to smile, but the corners of her mouth were stiff. "Sorry. I'm tired. But I'm fine."

"You look pale, like you're going to pass out. Are you sure you're all right? You should sit down. Here." His hand was still on her elbow, so he guided her gently but firmly down the row of books, to the end where there was an open space and a pair of upholstered chairs. Elisabeth privately referred to them as "the hideous chairs," as they were covered in a scratchy olive-green fabric, meant to last forever and never show stains.

At Shawn's urging, she sank down into a chair, and he sat opposite her.

"Half the kids at school are out with the flu. You might be coming down with something."

Elisabeth shook her head in alarm. The flu? Oh, no. That would be awful. A paper due, her paycheck, and Charlie—too many complications! The flu was not welcome, not now.

"I'm fine, just tired."

"I was looking for you down in the reference section. I know your American history class has a paper due tomorrow." Shawn cocked his head. "I thought you might be doing some last-minute research. But you're working instead."

Elisabeth flushed. Shawn was a peer tutor for the underclassmen, and American history was one of his areas. She didn't like to think maybe her teacher had noticed her complete lack of enthusiasm for the subject and had passed her name to Shawn. She hoped that wasn't the case.

"I didn't plan very well," she admitted. "But I'm not working too late tonight, just a couple of hours. And then I'll grab some books and get that paper done."

Shawn laughed in disbelief. "You haven't started?"

Elisabeth shook her head. "No," she admitted. "But research papers aren't hard for me. I'm sure I'll come up with something. I'll just be up until late tonight."

"Do you want some help? What are you writing on? Let me get the books for you."

Why was he being so nice? Elisabeth hesitated, not knowing what the right reply would be. This was Shawn Waterstone, Harvard-bound, blond and handsome, from a family that was not weird like hers. She'd only just spoken to him for the first time last week! Was this some kind of set-up? A practical joke? She'd heard about things like this, like when the football team hazed their freshman members by making them ask the ugliest girls in the school (based on a point-based scientific chart) out. Fortunately, she hadn't made the list of ugly girls, if only because no one ever remembered that she existed.

"I don't have a topic yet," she said. "I thought most of the books would be gone, since it's due tomorrow. I was going to take whatever books were left."

Shawn rose. "All right, then. Leave it to me. I know you're doing industrialization and factories. Late 1800s. I'll go see what's on the shelf."

"Thanks so much," Elisabeth said gratefully. "I really appreciate it. I might even get to bed at a decent hour."

"That's the goal," Shawn said. "Sleep is a good thing."

"But what about your own work?" Elisabeth asked, rising. "You're always studying. I see you here all the time." She blushed. Did he think she was watching him? Well, damn. She was, actually.

Just as she had feared, Shawn paused and looked at her. She glanced away, anything to avoid his inquiring gaze, then looked up again shyly, desperate to know what he was thinking.

But he said nothing, just beamed at her as if she'd given him a present. He turned and walked several rows down, gazing up at the signs that showed which numbers were in which row, before heading down one row and disappearing from sight.

He didn't need to check the catalogue, Elisabeth saw. He knew exactly where the American history books were, and he even knew which year was on which shelf. Well, that would make sense, wouldn't it? He wouldn't be destined for Harvard if he didn't know his way around a library.

Without warning, Charlie appeared at the far end of her aisle. When he saw her, he beamed and waved vigorously.

"Oh, jeez," Elisabeth groaned. Charlie looked completely out of place. He was well-dressed, with his woolen hat and neat boiled wool coat—probably much better dressed than most of his contemporaries—but his clothes looked quaint compared to what another boy his age in Greenleigh would be wearing. A well-dressed guy at school would wear a sweatshirt and maybe a parka, thought Elisabeth. Clunky work boots, as opposed to Charlie's slim leather boots, obviously handmade and expensive.

She tried to shoo him away by putting a finger to her lips and gesturing wildly, pointing behind him.

Puzzled, Charlie turned around. No one was there. The library wasn't busy tonight, and there wasn't even a lot of shelving to do. Elisabeth only had the one cart to finish, and she'd be able to grab her history books and leave. But she didn't want him to run into—

Shawn emerged from the stacks, carrying three thick books.

8

———

Elisabeth prayed silently, but it was no use. He saw Charlie right away and also saw that Charlie was grinning straight at Elisabeth.

The smile faded off Shawn's face as if he'd just been told that his dog had died. He stopped at the point where his aisle met the walkway, Charlie at one end, Elisabeth almost at the other in the hideous green chair. He stared hard at Charlie, then turned to look at Elisabeth.

In a moment, Elisabeth saw the truth. He liked her, she realized. It was like lightning, the realization that Shawn liked her. He liked her and had been waiting for her. He probably had been watching her over the past several weeks. Maybe even nervously getting up the courage to speak to her. And tonight, he'd made a point of coming into the stacks to find her. The offer to help her with her paper was an excuse. He just wanted to spend time with her.

She felt a conflicted tumult of feelings. On the one hand, she wanted to scream with joy, to float up to the ceiling on a cloud of happiness, to kick off her boots and slide around on the floor in her socks for the sheer glory of it.

When was the last time she had felt admired and liked for no reason other than the way in which she showed up in the world? Perhaps never?

On the other hand, there was a firm pressure in her chest, urging her to wrap her arms around herself to hold herself together, because surely this golden moment wouldn't last.

Because...Charlie.

"Who the hell is this guy?" Shawn's expression asked.

What do I tell him?

She shut her eyes for one moment, and when she opened them, Charlie had disappeared.

Shawn was turning to look at him again, but he had already slipped away. Shawn paused, then turned to walk slowly toward Elisabeth, his brow furrowed, clearly trying to figure out what he'd just seen, wondering how much he'd unwittingly let on.

"That was Charlie," Elisabeth said. She didn't know what else to say, but she had to say something.

"Charlie who?"

"Um—Charlie. Davis." Elisabeth held out her arms. "Thank you so much."

Absently, Shawn handed her the books. "There wasn't much there."

"Of course not. Everyone else has taken all the books. I'm late."

"Probably." Shawn rubbed his head with a hand. He was still frowning. Elisabeth knew that she ought to capitalize on her new realization, but she didn't quite know how, and she was wondering where Charlie had gone off to. Could she go check on him, she thought. Where could he have gone? Was he being an idiot and trying to chat up the librarians?

"He's kind of—silly," Elisabeth added, not knowing what else to say. How to explain Charlie? She couldn't possibly tell Shawn the truth.

"I was wondering," Shawn said. His voice was suddenly loud, as if he'd forgotten where he was. Elisabeth hastily put a finger to her lips, and he flushed. "Sorry," he whispered. "I was wondering if I could take you out after you finish up here."

"Oh! Oh. Um," Elisabeth began.

Crap! Obviously, the answer had to be no.

Was Shawn Waterstone asking her out? Was that what was happening?

"I've got this paper," she said lamely.

"I'll help you. It's not a long paper. More like an essay with citations. You can get it done. We can go to the Athena."

The Athena. The Greek diner at the highway interchange.

This really was a date, then. Shawn Waterstone was asking her out!

She looked up at him. A miserable pit was forming in her stomach.

"I can't," she said.

She tried to continue, but she couldn't get the words out of her throat. Shawn stared at her, waiting expectantly for her to continue.

Oh, my God. She'd just turned down a date with Shawn Waterstone.

She tried to think of something to say. How did one decline but ask for another chance at yes?

Suddenly, without warning, Charlie jumped out of the row of bookcases right next to them. He'd been hiding behind her cart of books. Elisabeth jumped and squeaked, dropping the three thick books on the floor with a deafening thud.

"Charlie!" she cried.

"Oh! Sorry, Beth!" He bent down to pick up the books but Shawn beat him to it. He straightened and put the books down on the table between the two hideous chairs.

"Shhhh!"

Down the aisle, an older woman in a brightly patterned sweater and long, dangling earrings was frowning at them. It was Tina Murphy, one of the librarians.

"I'm sorry," Charlie said in a whisper. He smiled, oozing charm, and the librarian's face softened. Elisabeth knew that she was fond of young people, and young men in particular, so Charlie was lucky.

"Is everything all right?" Tina asked, directing her question at Elisabeth.

"Yes," Elisabeth replied hastily. "I just dropped my books."

Tina nodded, her gaze traveling first to Shawn, then to Charlie, before she turned to leave.

Another person who'd seen Elisabeth with Charlie. Not good, Elisabeth thought.

"I'm Charlie." Charlie was holding his hand out to Shawn. Shawn hesitated for a moment before reaching out to shake his hand. Elisabeth closed her eyes in dismay. Teenaged boys weren't exactly known to shake hands. It was a good thing Shawn Waterstone was a step above most teenaged boys.

"Shawn."

"I'm a friend of Beth's."

This would not be a good conversation. She needed to interrupt it.

"I need to finish shelving my books before I can leave," Elisabeth said, rising. She turned to Shawn. "I wish I could, but I can't. Not tonight. I have to do this paper. I'm sorry."

Shawn was staring hard at Charlie. He turned his gaze back to Elisabeth. "Sure."

"Are—are you here for much longer?" She was trying to think of something else to say.

"I've got some calculus homework I'm trying to finish up. Not much longer, I guess."

"Oh."

For a moment, she just looked at him, feeling sorrier than she'd ever felt for herself. A date with Shawn Waterstone! And she'd just botched it.

And Charlie! He stood quietly in the aisle, pulling books out to examine them and putting them back. What was she going to do about Charlie? Three people in town had now seen her with him. Now, if she returned him to 1895, she'd have to make up a story about him.

"I'm going to get back to work," Shawn was saying. He touched her elbow. "Let me know if you need help with that paper. I'm here for a little while yet. And maybe we can hit the Athena next time."

"Yes!" she said, then felt embarrassed at how eager she sounded. She smiled. "Yes," she said again. "I'd like that."

He touched her elbow again. "Good," he said. He was watching her, and she found herself caught by his gaze. He was looking as if he were waiting for her to say something, but she didn't know what he might want her to say. She definitely couldn't say anything about Charlie. Was he waiting for her to explain his presence? Her heart beat faster.

Charlie's voice came from the stacks. He had moved further in, and he sounded as if he were bending over, possibly to look at something on a lower shelf.

"These are New England poets, Elisabeth!" He was trying to whisper, but the excitement in his voice made him hoarse.

Shawn turned, breaking eye contact with Elisabeth. His expression reverted to the perplexed and faintly hostile expression he'd reserved for Charlie. He looked back at Elisabeth. She shrugged, as if she didn't know what he was talking about.

Shawn knows I'm hiding something, she thought.

"I'll see you later," Shawn said. "We'll set a date for the Athena next time."

"Yes, please," Elisabeth replied. She tried to smile as he nodded and turned to go.

When he had turned the corner and was out of sight, she hurried back into the stacks. Charlie was sitting on the floor, surrounded by piles of books. He looked up, his eyes vacant and distracted.

"I've never heard of these people," he said. "But this is glorious."

Elisabeth bent over to look. A chill went down her spine. Well, he wouldn't have heard of Donald Hall or Jane Kenyon—and she didn't want to explain that they didn't yet exist in 1895. They were twentieth-century poets, much of their work from the 1970s and onward.

"This is wonderful," he continued. "Greenleigh doesn't have a library like this back where I come from. Or when I come from, rather."

"What about Linfield?" Elisabeth asked curiously.

He shook his head. "Not Linfield, either. There's a library in the next town. It's a subscription library, so you have to pay. There's a free library up north aways but I think only people who live there can use it."

"Then where do people get books?"

At this, Charlie scowled. He looked at the piles around him. "You don't know anything, do you? Aren't you listening to me?"

Taken aback, Elisabeth said, "What do you mean?"

Charlie sighed. "I keep trying to tell you. I didn't get to go to school, but Mary did. You get books at school. And Aunt Elisabeth has books. They're different, Aunt Elisabeth and Uncle Henry are. They have a lot of books just lying around the house. Most people can't get their hands on books at all. I can only get books because of Mary Elisabeth, and because of Aunt Elisabeth and Uncle Henry. My parents don't have many books, other than what my father buys for Mary."

There were old books all over the Burnham house, both downstairs and upstairs, and in boxes in the attic. Elisabeth suspected that the upper floor of the carriage house also held boxes of books. She knew it wasn't typical of people of the time to put so much money into books. But the Burnhams had money and education, and they'd lavished their resources on both their own immediate family and their extended family.

Charlie Davis, the boy who would eventually grow up to run the mill in Linfield, had been deprived of his wish to go to school. His family had the resources, but not the priorities. The only way for Charlie to get books was to steal his sister's poetry books and hide in the Burnham woodshed or sneak them off to the mill to read them during work hours.

She didn't want to feel sorry for Charlie. She knew that if she felt sorry for him, she would feel even worse than she already did about returning him to his own time. But she had to return him—he couldn't just leave his family. If even she wasn't prepared to ditch Mum and the Burnham house, he definitely would regret leaving Linfield and the mill, no matter how much he thought he wanted to be a poet. That much was clear. Seventeen-year-old boys shouldn't run away from home because of poetry.

She wondered if she could steal a moment to take a quick look at some local New England history books. Maybe she could figure out what the situation was with the Linfield Mill and use it to reason with him.

"Charlie," she whispered.

He didn't look up. He turned a page, seeming not to hear her. His lips moved. He frowned, then turned another page.

Elisabeth went back to her aisle. As soon as she was done, she thought, she was going to see what she could learn about Linfield and the mill.

9

———————

It didn't take long. After she had emptied the cart, she wheeled it back over to the service elevator where another cart was waiting, but it had only half a load, large format photography books of the coffee-table variety. She considered letting Charlie know where she was but decided against it. He was happy with his pile of poetry books and didn't seem interested in moving. If he needed her, he'd find her. And the library was quiet this evening, so no one was likely to come across him and start asking him questions.

The oversized book collection was the quietest section of the non-fiction area. Very few people took out these books, which were heavy and filled with specialized matter. The librarians often let these books pile up on a cart for a few weeks before returning them to the shelves, and Elisabeth rarely handled them. They were mostly older books, some of them from the sixties or seventies, with library bindings covered with crackly protective coverings that had once been crystal clear but were now yellowed with age.

She hoisted up the first book, a volume of Ansel Adams

photos. Elisabeth had never been interested in photography and did not feel herself to be artistic. Photos belonged in dusty old family albums, and when Daddy would pull them out, a boring story was sure to follow. And museums made her sleepy.

But the next book was entitled, "New England Landscapes," so she paused for a moment, examining the pretty Vermont scene on the cover, complete with Congregational church and covered bridge. It was the perfect tourist brochure photo, taken in the fall at the height of leaf-peeping season. She shelved this one more easily, as the shelf was at waist-level.

She picked up the next book. "Industrialization in New England Cities," she read. This was the subject of her as-yet-unwritten research paper, so she examined the book. The black-and-white photo on the cover was of a group of young women in dresses and aprons, staring solemnly at the camera.

These photographs dated back to the late 1800s, Elisabeth thought. She put it down on the cart in front of her because it was too heavy to hold up in her hands. She opened the book.

She flipped to the frontispiece where there was a photo-graph of a brick building next to a bridge over a stream. A horde of young boys leaned over the bridge, almost piled atop each other, grinning mischievously.

Would Charlie be in a picture like this, she wondered.

No, probably not. He wasn't a factory worker. His father owned the sawmill, which made him royalty. These were photos of mill workers, probably taken in Worcester or Lawrence. They were just young boys, maybe seven or eight years old, but already doing back-breaking, risky work. However, she realized that work was often the only choice for many. Even those who could afford it probably opted to earn money instead of spend money on education.

Her mind turned back to Charlie, even now sitting on the floor and mooning over poets he'd never heard of.

He couldn't stay in Greenleigh. It was impossible.

Wasn't it?

Elisabeth paused in the middle of turning a page. She stared into space. Then she shook her head.

No. It was ridiculous. There was nothing she could do to help him. She felt bad for him, but he couldn't just run away from his time and into hers. It wasn't right, and it would probably mess something up, cosmically speaking.

Absently, she flipped through the book in front of her. She wished she knew what the Davis family tree was all about, and how it intersected with her own. Did Charlie really end up running the mill? Had he miserably agreed to the path set for him, following out the destiny that wasn't his to decide?

She suddenly stopped, then peered closely at the page in front of her.

A group of men in fancy suits and hats posing with ladies on their arms. The ladies wore their own hats with outrageous feathers and trimmings, jewels and gowns. In the background was—

Elisabeth squinted. She leaned back, angling the book under the buzzing fluorescent fixture overhead. She couldn't quite make out the grainy faces in the image, but the building in back looked familiar. It looked like the group was posed on the front steps of a theater or music hall.

She couldn't be sure, but it looked like the decrepit old theater in downtown Greenleigh, which was declared a firetrap and scheduled for demolition years ago. Because the local historical society had gotten the state and national historic preservation organizations involved in efforts to preserve the old theater, the demolition order was locked in a court battle, and the old building still stood vacant.

There was nothing interesting in the caption, no names, but the date was 1900, and one of the couples was young, very young. She couldn't make out the faces, but the stiff posture reminded her of Charlie in the shed, when he'd figured out that something was up about the overhead light and had turned his face upwards.

The young woman was lifting her chin in a defiant pose, and her hands gripped hard at the young man's arm. She had dark hair and a hat with ostrich plumes, but that was all Elisabeth could make out. Her face was a mere smudge.

It was the man's posture, the tilt of his upraised head, that struck her. It looked for all the world like Charlie.

But he was not the cheerful young man sprawled out on the Greenleigh library floor reading poetry. And there was something odd about his stance, about the way he was standing. Almost as if he were leaning against the young woman for support.

Elisabeth turned back to the title page of the book. "Industrialization," she mused. Then she turned back to the photo, hoping that the pause in her scrutiny had helped to clear her eyesight, and that this time she might see better.

Nope. The faces were still blurry and grainy. All that she could be sure of was that the group was standing in front of a public building, dressed in their finest, and that the young man off to one side seemed tense. The caption did not identify the building, but the photographer's name was—

Drew Clark.

A rush of recognition came over her. Drew Clark was a photographer who'd grown up in Greenleigh and was well known for his turn of the century portraiture. His had been one of the other grand old houses on Church Street. He'd remained unmarried and had left Greenleigh for greater parts, eventually becoming famous and dying a rich man somewhere in New York City, with obituaries published in all the big papers. His house was passed down to a niece or a nephew but was eventually sold and wasn't in the family anymore. Whoever was living in it now had done a huge rehab, and Elisabeth had heard that it was scooped out like a melon and gutted completely, and looked like a fancy Boston condo inside, complete with a jacuzzi and pool out back. She'd never seen the inside of the house, but she'd heard about it from the church ladies, who were scandalized at the ostentatious spending and the wasteful modernization of a perfectly good interior. Elisabeth wasn't too sure she agreed with that perspective but had never put any thought into the topic.

The Greenleigh library had a ton of resources on Drew Clark. She wondered if she could find out what had happened to the Linfield Mill and to the Davis family by looking at Drew Clark photos. There were Clark portraits of her own Burnham ancestors here and there in the attic, most of them posed in front of the house. Drew Clark liked to photograph his subjects in front of their workplace or with the tools of their trade, but he was also a highly compensated portrait photographer for the wealthy. There was even a photograph of Judge Burnham in front of the courthouse, looking stern. Daddy had said he'd objected to the portrait, feeling that it was inappropriate and needlessly vain for a public servant to pose for a photograph. But Grammy had insisted, saying that one day their Burnham great-grandchildren would want to see Grampy at his place of work. That portrait was propped up in the parlor, covered with spider webs and dust. It had fallen down behind a couch at some point, and she'd hauled it out from underneath and cleaned up the broken glass but hadn't known what to do with it. Mum certainly didn't care about any of the Burnham relations, that was for sure.

At any rate, Elisabeth guessed that if she could find collections of Clark portraits, she would find photos of the Linfield Mill, and there would be people in those photos.

She replaced the books on the shelves in record time, not

quite sure if she'd gotten them all into the right place. For once, she didn't dawdle and leaf through the books, but returned the cart to the service elevator and headed to the reference section.

How would she look up photographs? She didn't have the faintest idea.

10

———————

"Are you done, Beth dear?" Mrs. Murphy looked up from her desk. Elisabeth saw that she had shadows under her eyes, and that she'd tried to camouflage them with a thick layer of makeup. Mrs. Miller had whispered at church that Mrs. Murphy was going through financial hardship, that her husband was an alcoholic, that he kept getting laid off because of "the bottle." Elisabeth hadn't been sure of what "the bottle" was until she'd seen Mr. Murphy on the street one day, staggering and shouting incoherently at passers-by.

She wondered if Mrs. Murphy ever wanted to disappear into another century. She snuck a quick look at the book she'd laid aside on her desk. It looked like a children's book.

She understands the urge to hide, Elisabeth thought. *If you can't run, then hide.*

"Mrs. Murphy, I'm all done now. I have to write a paper by tomorrow so I'm doing some research. Can you tell me how to find old photographs taken by Drew Clark?"

"Drew Clark? The photographer? Oh, my. Well, some of his work was compiled and made into books after he died in the fifties. Are you into photography, Beth?" Mrs. Murphy had risen and was making her way over to a terminal. "Let me put some keywords in here."

"Thanks, Mrs. Murphy. No, I don't know much about photography. I'm looking for his earlier work. The work he did in and around Greenleigh."

"Here you go, then." There was a small pile of neatly cut scratch paper and a pen on a chain next to the terminal. Mrs. Murphy scribbled on a sheet of paper, then handed it to Elisabeth. "These are in storage. There are at least a dozen books with his work in them, more or less catalogued under the same numbers."

"That's great," Elisabeth exclaimed. "Thank you so much."

Mrs. Murphy smiled a little sadly and shook her head, her brightly colored earrings swinging. "You're such a good girl, Beth. How's your mother? Any better this week?"

"Uh—not really, Mrs. Murphy. The same."

"I feel for her. It must be hard," Mrs. Murphy said. She paused, absently stroking an earring, then seemed to shake herself out of a daze. She smiled at Elisabeth. "You know, Shawn Waterstone was asking about you. He likes you."

Elisabeth felt herself flush. She felt dizzy for a moment, not knowing what to say.

"I hope you don't mind. I told him I've known you forever. Since you were a little girl."

"Oh," Elisabeth said weakly.

"He's a nice boy. And not a bit shy." Mrs. Murphy laughed. "He made it clear that he wanted to get to know you. I teased him a little, and he didn't mind. He said he's been watching you and he wants to ask you out but thought you might have a boyfriend."

"A boyfriend!" Elisabeth gasped. She giggled in spite of herself. "I guess you told him I don't have a boyfriend, Mrs. Murphy!"

"Why shouldn't you have a boyfriend, Beth?" Mrs. Murphy sounded severe. She leaned forward, put her hand on Elisabeth's arm. "You're in that big old house with your mum. You must feel like you're alone. You should spend some time with kids your age. Have some fun."

Elisabeth nodded, but she felt sure Mrs. Murphy couldn't possibly know what the school crowd was like. She'd long since gotten used to eating lunch alone and skipping all the social events at school, but most people wouldn't know that this was the only way she could stand to keep going. Socializing was work. Smiling was work. Getting out of bed was work.

"Are you worried because he's a senior?"

Elisabeth looked at her blankly. She shrugged. She wasn't sure what Mrs. Murphy meant. Did it make a difference that Shawn Waterstone was seventeen and she was fifteen?

Mrs. Murphy added, "He's not going far. Harvard's not even two hours away. And he's an only son. He'll be back to visit all the time. Vacations and summers. You'd see him often."

Ah. Elisabeth understood now. Mrs. Murphy thought she might not want to date someone who was leaving town and might never come back.

If she could leave Greenleigh, she wasn't at all sure that she would come back.

"He's only two years older than you," Mrs. Murphy was still talking. "He says he doesn't plan to run his father's factory, but I think he'll change his mind. Eventually."

Elisabeth paused. She turned to Mrs. Murphy. "Factory?"

"Yes, his family owns Mountainview Wool Company. On the edge of town. You've heard of it, I'm sure."

Elisabeth nodded, but her mind was considering something else. A factory! Shawn's family owned a factory, just the way Charlie's did. And Shawn was an only child who had no plans to stay in Greenleigh to run a family business.

The parallels were a strange coincidence.

Charlie wasn't an only child, however. He had a sister, although she didn't seem interested in the business. In 1895, perhaps girls didn't inherit businesses, Elisabeth thought.

She wondered if Charlie's sister was also eager to leave. She'd been to school, so she'd had some experience outside of Linfield.

Was this feeling of choking claustrophobia normal, then? This sense that there was something more than old wood stoves and green wood that wouldn't light? Parents who didn't notice you and church ladies who did—a little too much?

"Thank you so much for this, Mrs. Murphy." Elisabeth held up the slip of paper. "I'll go check storage for these books."

"You've very welcome." Mrs. Murphy smiled a little wistfully. "I hope you give Shawn a chance. Such a sweet boy."

Elisabeth surprised herself by replying. "I will." Mrs. Murphy beamed before turning to retreat once more to her desk.

Elisabeth hurried back to the stacks. Charlie was still exactly where she had left him, sitting on the floor and surrounded by books. He didn't bother to look up when she appeared.

"Charlie, I need to go downstairs into the cellar to grab some books. Do you want to come with me? Or would you rather wait here?"

"I'll wait," he said, his voice distant.

Elisabeth hesitated. Maybe she should bring him with her.

"You know, I think you should come with me. You can bring books with you. Just grab a couple. We'll put the rest of these away when we come back."

Charlie turned a page. He appeared not to have heard her. Elisabeth waited a moment, then spoke a little louder.

"Charlie."

His lips were moving, but he did not look up. She reached out and gave his arm a little shake.

"Come with me, Charlie."

No reply.

She had an idea. "You've never been in an elevator, I'll bet."

He looked up. "A what?"

"Come with me. You'll see."

He looked around irritably, his eyes still unfocused. "I was just in the middle of this poem."

"Come on, you can leave the books there, we'll come back in a few minutes. I just thought you'd like to ride the elevator." She went to the end of the row and peered down the adjacent corridor. There was a cart parked at the end of one of the other rows, so she went over to grab it and roll it over to where Charlie was sitting.

"Look, we can put these books on the cart. That way we can find them when we get back."

Grumpily, Charlie scrambled to his feet, and together they put the books on the cart. Elisabeth counted sixteen different books, both volumes of poetry and biographies of poets. She breathed a sigh of relief that Charlie had not yet penetrated the biographies, most of which were of poets who weren't yet born in the 1890s. He probably didn't realize when any of the poems he was reading were written, and he probably wasn't checking the publication dates of the books, either.

"What are you going down to the cellar for?" Charlie asked. He seemed muted, preoccupied.

"I need to get some books from storage and I didn't want you to worry if you didn't find me anywhere. Did you enjoy the poetry books?"

"Yeah. Do you like poetry?"

"Not much," Elisabeth confessed.

"You know, Aunt Elisabeth loves poetry." Charlie was silent

for a moment. Then he added, "She would be amazed at this library. At those books. She had a lot of books. But there are so many more here. And so many poetry books."

Elisabeth waved at Mrs. Murphy as they passed the reference desk. Mrs. Murphy smiled and nodded, gazing curiously first at Charlie, then at Elisabeth.

"Maybe we should tell people we're cousins or something," Elisabeth muttered after they were out of earshot.

"We pretty much are," Charlie replied.

"Do you know where in the family tree we're related?"

"No. Someone is married to someone but I don't know who. Aunt Elisabeth has always been Aunt Elisabeth. And my mum is her best friend. They grew up together and went to school together. I think I told you that."

"I wish I knew," Elisabeth muttered.

Charlie shrugged. "It don't matter. Who's the guy, Shawn?"

Elisabeth shook her head. "Just a guy. I know him from school."

"Well, he looked daggers at me. Hey! Is this the whatsit?" Charlie bounded ahead toward the service elevator.

"Go ahead and press that button," Elisabeth said.

Charlie obeyed. There was a loud groan in the distance as the elevator began its ascent, and he stepped back slightly in alarm. When the doors began to open, he stepped back yet again, but Elisabeth grabbed his arm and led him in. She motioned to the button with the "B" and Charlie pressed it. After a long moment, the doors creaked shut, and he looked around once, wild-eyed.

"You're sure this is all right?" he said nervously.

"I've ridden this thing hundreds of times," Elisabeth replied. "It's fine. It's actually slower and sturdier than the regular elevator for the public. That one sometimes gets finicky. Sometimes it stops working and people have to take the stairs, the way we did in the front of the building. And they get furious, because they're carrying a heavy load of books. But this one is for staff, and it's always working."

"Huh," Charlie grunted. He still looked uncomfortable, twitching at every screech and groan. Finally, when the doors opened, he darted out into the darkened corridor. In a moment, the lights flickered on, and he jumped.

"The lights go on automatically," Elisabeth said, trying not to laugh. The smile left her face when she saw Charlie's expression. Poor guy. He was scared. And why shouldn't he be, she thought. This must all look like witchcraft.

"Here, I'm going this way," she said quickly. "There's no one down here at night. And we don't have to whisper."

Charlie was clinging to her elbow without any sense of embarrassment.

"I don't like this floor," he muttered. As they walked along, lights flickered on overhead, row by row.

"It's a little spooky," Elisabeth agreed sympathetically. She didn't tell him she enjoyed being in the storage area because it was so silent, her ears hurt.

"I wish you'd left me upstairs. And I don't like the—the—thing we rode in. I don't want to go in there again."

"All right. There are stairs. Gosh, Charlie. I thought you'd enjoy it. I'm sorry. I guess I wasn't thinking." Elisabeth was contrite.

"Naw. Not your fault. This is just strange."

"Ready to go home, then?"

"Naw," Charlie said again, more boldly. "I liked those books upstairs. Where does your friend Shawn go to school?"

They were walking toward the back of the room, where the oversized books were stored. Elisabeth consulted the scratch paper in her hand for a moment, then nodded.

"The books I want are on that shelf right along the back wall."

"Do you think I could just live with you and go to school with Shawn?"

"It's not that easy, Charlie," Elisabeth said gently. In spite of herself, she wondered if Charlie had enough math to be in a twentieth-century high school. Had math changed at all since the nineteenth century? Certainly he wouldn't know enough history or science. And literature—she thought she'd read that English wasn't even a field of study until the twentieth century. But he read poetry, she conceded. Maybe he could survive high school English?

Mentally, she shook herself. What was this bizarre line of thinking? He was dragging her into an argument that didn't make any sense. He wasn't going to school in Greenleigh, period.

As they reached the back row of books, Charlie stopped. He faced her and said earnestly, "I want to be where the books are, Beth. How do I do that? How can I be where the books are?"

For a long moment, they looked at each other, Charlie's expression pleading.

"You can't stay here, Charlie," Elisabeth said finally. "I can't explain you turning up at school. Even if you were to live with us and Mum never found out—which is entirely possible, I'll admit that—the school would insist on talking to your parents. Someone would have to do paperwork to put you in school. It's just—I can't even explain how confusing all of this would be. It just wouldn't work. It's stupid. I think it's a stupid system. But I can't explain why it's this way, it's just that it is this way."

Charlie's shoulders slumped. His face fell. Then he straightened again, and said a little defiantly, "All right. I'll work. And I'll study on the side. I'll read the books in this here library. I can do that."

"But Charlie! You could do that at home!" pleaded Elisabeth.

"Your parents will be sick with worry about you. Don't you feel terrible about your parents? Just think how upset they must be."

Charlie scowled. "They're not that upset."

"But they want you to take over the mill! What will happen to the mill with you gone?"

"Father's got lots of guys who could take over the mill. Or he could sell it." Charlie stood for a moment, his thumbs hooked into the pockets of his coat. Then he aimed a vicious kick at the wall in front of them.

Elisabeth winced. "Don't. I understand. I'll try to think of something, some way to help."

"You can't help," Charlie said bitterly. "Unless you let me stay here with you. If I go back, I'm stuck at that mill."

"Your sister—she could run the mill?" Elisabeth said tentatively.

Charlie let out a crow of laughter. "Mary Elisabeth? Are you kidding me? She hates it as much as I do. She's got a guy—" He suddenly stopped and clamped his lips shut.

"A guy? She's seeing someone?"

"Aw heck," Charlie muttered. "I wasn't supposed to say. Sometimes I tease her about it, but she'll get into real trouble if anyone finds out."

"Don't worry," Elisabeth said hastily. "I can't possibly tell anyone who would get her into trouble. Right?"

Charlie relaxed. "Yeah. Yeah, I guess so." He hesitated, then continued. "Mary's been seeing a man who's a lot older. He's got two small boys. And if Father and Mother found out—"

Elisabeth gasped. Charlie looked up at her. Then he suddenly grabbed her arm.

"Wait a minute. Just wait a minute here. You know something, don't you? You know what happens to Mary!"

11

"I don't—" Elisabeth protested, but it was no use. Charlie had grabbed both her arms. He shook her lightly.

"Tell me," he begged. "Tell me what happens. Does Mary marry this guy? Am I going to run that mill? Maybe there's no use to anything I might do. Maybe I'm just stuck. Or—did I disappear? Maybe I never went back to Linfield. Maybe I'll never find my way back. Did my father sell the mill?" He shook her again. "Beth, if you know something—tell me!"

"I don't know anything," she gasped.

But she did. She had connected Charlie's sister Mary Elisabeth with a cousin Mary of Burnham family lore. Yes, she married a man with two small boys. And her husband ended up beating her until she fled. By that time, the man—Dietrich Behr, a teacher of German at the fancy academy for ladies that Mary had attended for several years—had emptied her bank account and sold much of her jewelry to feed his gambling habit.

Behr's children by his first wife had died in a mysterious accident involving a fall down a flight of cellar stairs. Her dad had told her this tale more than once as a ghost story. The house where the accident happened was across the street and down aways, a wreck of an old home with an unkempt front lawn, and Elisabeth had never been able to look at the house without a shudder. It looked and felt like a cursed house. In the back of her mind, she associated wrecked old colonials with ongoing curses of family that wouldn't let its claws out of you.

Behr had drunk himself to death, her father had said. Mary had taken the two little boys back home with her, and that was where the fascinating story had ended. The house across the street, which Behr had been renting, stayed vacant for a long time afterward. No one wanted to live in a house that had seen that much ill fortune. It was the site of the local food pantry nowadays, supported by an interdenominational church council and a lot of community donations.

So that was why Mary Elisabeth wanted to visit with the Burnhams! She was secretly meeting Dietrich Behr. Elisabeth tried not to shudder. She hadn't realized that the woman in the ghost story whom she'd always known as "Mary-Bear" was actually Mary Elisabeth Behr, a Davis. She certainly hadn't realized that she was Charlie's sister. And she hadn't realized that this cautionary tale was right in Charlie's immediate future. If her rapid-fire mental calculations were correct, Mary Elisabeth would run away with Dietrich Behr within the year. She would quit school. She would shock her parents and the surrounding community.

And they would all be counting on Charlie, presumably, to step up and take care of things. Not to become a poet, but to become the head of the family business that would keep Mary Elisabeth going when she eventually fled her violent husband.

But how could she possibly tell Charlie this story?

"I don't know anything," she repeated, but it was too late. Charlie was staring at her hard, waiting expectantly to hear her reply.

"Look, Charlie," she began.

"Don't lie to me, Beth," he begged. "This is me, Charlie. Don't lie to me. We're kin, right?"

They were, Elisabeth thought. They were kin, she and Charlie. She'd never felt a tremendous amount of affinity for the Burnhams, but Charlie was a boy her age, a boy with dreams who would shortly be presented with a family crisis. And he was kin.

No, no. That wasn't right. Her mother was family, not Charlie. Charlie was a ghost! Her mother was her "real" kin. Even if she couldn't look after her right now, even if she'd never been happy with her father, even if she'd never been happy with Elisabeth.

Elisabeth tried to shut out the instant feeling of shame that washed over her as thoughts of her mother entered her mind.

She'd never really thought about "kin" before. She'd never considered what it felt like to be connected to anyone besides Mum and Dad. Dad had been a terrible provider, but he'd been a kind father. His stories were the only thing that connected her to the people in his past. Judge Burnham, his father. Great-Uncle Alfred, who'd died in the war but left a big bank account, the one that Grampy had inherited and had eventually ended up as the trust fund that Dad had lived on. Cousin Mildred. Great-Aunt Eugenia. And all the Elisabeths. There were countless Elisabeths in the family bible. All of them spelled with an "s." The "s" that told you exactly what the Burnhams were like. Quirky. Odd. Difficult.

She scarcely knew anything about her mother's family in Vermont, except that they hadn't wanted her to marry James Burnham. That was probably another entire rabbit trail of family ghosts and skeletons in the closet.

"I just want to look at some of these books," she muttered. She consulted the slip of paper in her hand, then pulled out a volume from the shelf of oversized books.

She flipped through the first few pages, but it clearly wasn't what she was looking for. It was a compilation of New England photographers, and Drew Clark had two photographs toward the end of the book, in the section called "Industry." These were architectural photos, and she wondered what on earth he was doing photographing buildings, when his genius lay in environmental portraits of people in their contexts. Well, artists had to eat, she supposed.

She put the book back, consulted her scrap of paper again.

Charlie was standing, hands on hips, waiting for a reply, his posture stiff and angry. He wanted to know about Mary. She didn't look at him but felt his eyes on her as she pulled another book out. This was another heavy book, a coffee-table book.

Drew Clark: A Life in Portraits.

This would be his body of work. Curated by—whom? A beloved friend or colleague? An art historian working on her dissertation? A family member?

She flipped to the first page. Publication date in the 1950s, either near the end of his life or after his death. Author...

...Elisabeth Burnham.

She gave a little gasp and shut the book.

"What is it?" Charlie cried. He jumped forward to snatch the book out of her hands, but she tugged it away viciously, holding it high above her head. It was heavy, so she wobbled, barely able to keep it out of Charlie's reach.

"No!" She backed away, shaking her head. "No! Stop!"

"Let me see!" Charlie said, once again lunging for the book, but she stepped back again.

"Stop it, Charlie! I need to see this!"

"What did you see?"

"I don't know yet! Let me be, Charlie!"

She plunked herself down on the floor, then opened the

book again. Charlie sat down beside her but did not make another move to grab the book. He stared at her hard.

"Go on," he whispered. "Go on, then. But don't be stingy. Tell me what's in there."

She flipped carefully through the first few pages. There was a dedication. "To the best man in the world, my father." There was a faded portrait above those words, but it was just a photograph of some old guy in a suit, looking dapper. That would be —who? It told her nothing new. He looked familiar, but that wouldn't be strange if he was a Burnham. The original of the photo was probably somewhere in the attic, in an album.

Elisabeth frowned, thinking. She needed to tease out her connection to these people. She could do this—it wasn't all that long ago, in the same century, in fact. She just had to do it quietly, without Charlie figuring it out himself.

Mentally, she recited what she knew. Charlie and his sister Mary were living in 1895. Charlie was seventeen, Mary was probably close to twenty. They were visiting their Aunt Elisabeth Burnham in Greenleigh. Aunt Elisabeth was a close friend of their mother. They had been schoolmates, so they were the same age.

How old was Aunt Elisabeth, she wondered?

She asked Charlie, "How old is your Aunt Elisabeth?"

"What?" Charlie said. "How old is she? I don't know."

"She's your mother's age."

"Yes. My mother had her forty-second birthday last summer. It was here, in fact." Charlie gestured around them, although they were at the moment sitting on the floor, surrounded by books, in the Greenleigh Public Library. "I mean, it was at Aunt Elisabeth's house. Because Mother didn't want a birthday in Linfield. She wanted a garden party, so Aunt Elisabeth threw her a garden party."

For a moment, Charlie's face had softened as he remembered. Elisabeth knew exactly what a garden party in the house's backyard would have looked like. And she could imagine why someone from Linfield would have wanted a genteel Greenleigh party. She'd only ever driven through Linfield on the way up north, but it had a quiet downtown and a grubby set of brick industrial buildings out on the edge of town. Elisabeth had never paid much attention on the odd occasion when her father mentioned the Linfield relatives. She regretted it now, wondering what he could have told her about the Davises.

Charlie said, "Why do you want to know?"

Elisabeth shook herself. She just couldn't remember anything that Daddy might have told her about the Davises, and it frustrated her to no end. Nothing that he had said seemed extraordinary or interesting. She remembered the scary stories about Dietrich Behr, but that wasn't about the Davises. Well, it sort of wasn't.

She pushed the thought of Mary Elisabeth out of her mind. She couldn't think about poor Mary Elisabeth now. She needed to figure out Charlie first.

And Elisabeth Burnham! Who was she, this Elisabeth Burnham who catalogued photographs of New England in the 1950s? There was no foreword, no note in the book that might tell them. She had to be a relative, but that was all they could assume.

It's 1995, Elisabeth thought. *Forty years have passed. She's probably dead.*

"Listen to me, Beth." Charlie spoke quickly, earnestly. He reached out as if to take one of her hands, then stopped awkwardly as she pulled the book away protectively. "I need you to listen to me," he repeated.

"Charlie, I'm listening," Elisabeth said. "But—"

"No, you don't understand," he said. "I've been thinking for a long time. Thinking about leaving all of it behind. The mill. Mother and Father. All of it. Linfield. New England."

12

———

"What? But—but Charlie—" Elisabeth gasped.

Charlie was staring down at his hands, which he was now clasping and unclasping in his lap. For the first time, Elisabeth noticed how rough and calloused his palms were, how his hands were the hands of a worker, not a scholar.

"Where would you go? What would you do?"

"I'd go west," he said. "To Chicago, or maybe even to California. I'm sick of all of this. Mary's sick of it, too, I know she is. That's why she took up with that guy. We're so tired of Linfield."

"Charlie, listen to me," Elisabeth begged. "If you do that, you'll end up working even harder and reading even less poetry than you do now."

"Tell me honestly," Charlie implored. "Why shouldn't I leave home? I'm so tired of it all. Father is always getting after me to run the parts of the factory that are giving him trouble. They're rough men, Beth. They drink and mess around, and the equipment is dangerous. I don't like that world. I don't like it one bit. I want to read books, maybe teach in a school someday. I don't want to run a sawmill. I don't care how much money it makes or how important Father is. Don't you ever think about leaving? Don't you ever tire of your life? Do you want to just do the things everyone else expects you to do? Have you never thought of what else you could do, if only you were free to do it?"

"Oh, Charlie," Elisabeth said, sighing. She put down the book. "If only you knew. Yes, of course I think about that. I think about it a lot. But you know, I am who I am. I'll never leave Greenleigh. I can't. What would I do?"

"There must be a million things you could do!" Charlie exclaimed. "You're living in a future I can't even imagine—lights that go on when you walk into rooms, horseless carriages, and endless free books, everywhere you look! You want to send me back to a place where I'll probably lose a couple fingers before I'm thirty. If I'm lucky! We've had men cut their legs off, their arms, bleed to death. Some of them drink their pay before payday, and then we have to tell their wives there's no money that week. Their babies are crying with hunger. I don't want that life, Beth. I'll do anything to get out of it."

"I don't want that life for you, either," Elisabeth protested. "But I don't know what I can do about it. I don't even know if I can return you back to your life properly. All we know is that you did it through the shed. You might be stuck here, anyway."

"I might be," Charlie conceded. "And if I am, then we must assume that God wants me to be here."

Elisabeth hesitated. She had no right to keep information from him if she knew it. She couldn't bring herself to talk about Mary. That seemed wrong—almost private, somehow. Mary needed to make her own choices, and whatever Charlie knew should be the extent to which she wanted to share. But Drew Clark—

"This book is filled with photographs taken by Drew Clark. Have you heard of him?"

Charlie shook his head. Elisabeth opened the book to the

title page and held it up for him to inspect. Charlie leaned over. He looked at the dedication page and shook his head over the portrait, but when he caught sight of the author's name, his eyes widened.

"Lord," he whispered. "But that can't be you. That book's older than you are."

"I don't know who this is," she said. "This book was published in the 1950s. I guess if I looked at the family Bible I could figure this out. I would have to go digging around in the attic for it, because my father was not religious, and he didn't want it downstairs. I don't know which Elisabeth Burnham this is, but it doesn't fit with your Aunt Elisabeth. It's at least two generations beyond her."

"That makes it one generation past me, then."

Elisabeth nodded. "Yes."

"But Aunt Elisabeth doesn't have children. She married late, Mother said. That's why she's so good to me and Mary."

"Then she's a cousin? Or maybe a completely different Burnham family? I doubt it, because Drew Clark took lots of photographs around Greenleigh."

Elisabeth carefully turned the beginning pages of the book. There were photographs of street life, farm life. Portraits of merchants, shopkeepers, businessmen. The town hall was naked without its belfry, which was a later addition. Charlie watched her go through each page, methodically scanning the captions.

"Whoever this Elisabeth Burnham was, she was focused on Drew Clark's evolution as an artist," Elisabeth said. "These photographs are more or less in chronological order, and you can see how he developed. And the technology changed, too."

"Are we related to him?"

"I don't think so," Elisabeth said. "I don't remember ever hearing about him at home, from my dad. He would have bragged about having a famous photographer in the family, if we were related."

"Then why did she write this book?"

"That's a good question," Elisabeth admitted. "And I've never heard of her. I don't even know if she's from Greenleigh."

"But she spells her name like yours," Charlie pointed out. "And Aunt Elisabeth does, too. My father always said it was those damned Burnhams, having to do things different." He flushed, then muttered, "Sorry about the swearing."

"That's okay," Elisabeth said, smiling. "You're funny, Charlie Davis. You have no idea how kids ours age talk nowadays."

"Hey. Hold on one second. Can you turn that page back?"

Elisabeth obeyed. The photograph in question was of a ramshackle wooden structure with a horse tied to a post beside it. A small boy grinned broadly into the camera. He was shirtless, with ripped, dirty trousers, and had one hand placed protectively on the horse's neck. The weeds and scrubby growth around the wooden building indicated a level of neglect and poverty that seemed out of sync with most of the photographs at the beginning of the book.

"I know him!" Charlie exclaimed. "That's Johnny Hudson! And that horse there is Cricket!"

"Is this Linfield?"

"No, that's Greenleigh. I just know that boy. His father wasn't around much—he was a peddler—and Johnny used to come by once in a while with things to sell. But they lived on the edge of Greenleigh proper. I don't even know whose land that is. I don't think they were farmers."

Elisabeth tried not to shudder. What a borderline existence. "So he's about your age?"

Charlie averted his eyes. "Was. Johnny's dead."

"Oh! Oh, no. What happened to him?"

"I don't know for sure. What I heard was that they had to sell

Cricket. And Johnny kicked up a big fuss. His dad beat him, but Johnny wouldn't listen. So he tried to run away with Cricket, but he got lost in a snowstorm. They found him in the spring. I don't know what happened. Maybe he froze to death, maybe he was hiding out somewhere and got sick." Charlie shrugged uncomfortably.

"That's horrible," Elisabeth gasped. Together, they bent over the photograph of Johnny and Cricket. The lively light in Johnny's eyes, coupled with his affectionate stance toward his horse, made the story of his demise feel even worse than it was.

"Yeah," Charlie said. "It happens."

"This doesn't happen anymore, Charlie."

"Really? How's that?"

Elisabeth shook her head. She flipped a page and tried to speak normally, but her throat was choked with emotion. Children freezing outdoors—this didn't happen in twentieth-century America. Did it? If it did, she preferred not to know. It seemed that for Charlie, this wasn't a strange occurrence.

Who would willingly return to that world?

The next several pages showed more formal portraits. As Drew Clark went forward with his career, he was gaining more commissions from people who could afford to pay him. The captions written by Elisabeth Burnham showed that he was fond of his "environmental portraits" of people and places around Greenleigh, but some commissioned portraits were taking place further afield. Factory owners in Lowell, Lawrence, and Worcester were having family portraits taken, and when Clark went traveling outside of Greenleigh, he would capture the life of ordinary New Englanders by photographing the workforce in front of the buildings and equipment. There were photographs of children in ragged shirts and aprons, women standing in front of looms twice their size, and rough-looking men who glared at the camera, hands on hips, with grease stains on their arms and faces. The author explained that Clark claimed to the factory owners that he wanted to document the expansion of their premises and operations, but in fact, he was interested in what people did for work and how they felt about it. He would take formal portraits of the factory owners and their families, then find a pretense to explore the factories themselves.

The portraits of children in pristine white dresses, standing in beautiful rose gardens with their nannies and their toys, disturbed Elisabeth when she considered the children in the factories who seemed barely old enough to run errands on the factory floor. She felt that Drew Clark was saying something without saying it. That he persisted in photographing people in their workaday context while funding his work through commissions from the wealthy seemed to speak volumes. The further she went in the book, the more dramatic the gap appeared. There were fewer casual photographs like the one of Jimmy and Cricket, and more photographs of factory owners and their families in their Sunday finest.

She flipped forward several more pages, not bothering to check the captions. She didn't know what she was looking for, but this wasn't it. She had thought she might find some family history in these pages, but the Burnhams weren't industrialists. They were scholars and professionals in the law. Their sort would not have interested Drew Clark or the Elisabeth Burnham who was doing the compilation. That photograph of Grampy in the parlor, Elisabeth realized, was out of character for Clark. It was probably a money-maker, an attempt to fund the social commentary that he loved, the traveling that thrilled him. Where was that photograph of the group of wealthy theater goers? It wasn't in this collection. That young man had looked so much like Charlie, she thought.

And then, suddenly, she found something.

She was turning pages rapidly when she saw it. The burned-out husk of a building. The brick foundations were still there, but otherwise it was a blackened dirt lot.

"Linfield Mill, 1898," read the caption. "Destroyed by fire, caught on film several weeks later."

Horrified, Elisabeth stared at the image. Charlie, who had been moodily drumming his fingers against the bookcase next to them, leaned over to look. He stiffened.

"That's the mill," he breathed.

Elisabeth turned to look at the previous page, but there was no text leading up to the photograph.

"Let me see that." Numbly, Elisabeth passed the book to Charlie, who scrutinized the image. In one corner, a little boy stood with a stick in his hands, next to an old man with a mustache. The old man had one hand placed firmly on the boy's shoulder as he stared into the camera.

"Do you know them?" Elisabeth whispered.

Charlie shook his head. "Nope. They look like maybe they're scavenging. Looking for metal scraps." He turned the page. "Does it say when this happened? What season?"

"It doesn't look like winter in that photograph," Elisabeth said. "It's probably later in the year."

Together, they scanned several pages, but there was no mention of time of year, and no further mention of what had happened to the mill, the family who owned it, or the workers.

"Nothing," Charlie said.

"I can find out," Elisabeth said. She started to rise. "There'll be newspaper articles. This has to be big news for Linfield, and even for Greenleigh. And—and records of what happened to—" She couldn't get the words out.

Charlie stood up with her. He seemed numb. He shook his head. "I don't know what to think. Do Father and the other men die? Do I die? In that fire?"

Elisabeth shook her head. If she made him go back to his own time, was she sentencing him to death? If he stayed here in Greenleigh, would he be forever haunted by the knowledge that he had perhaps avoided a terrifying fate, and left others to face what he had escaped?

"I don't know what to say, Charlie. The Linfield Mill exists today, so it had to have been rebuilt. Maybe this terrible tragedy didn't affect your family as badly as it could have. Maybe no one died."

Charlie was shaking his head. "I don't know if I want to know," he whispered. His face was ashen. "But how can I go back now, knowing even this much? That the mill is going to burn down?"

"I'm so sorry, Charlie," Elisabeth said. She felt the impossibility of his predicament, and she held out her arms to him. He reached out to hug her tightly. He was so thin, she thought. Skin and bone and muscle. For all his wisecracking, he was just a boy.

She now realized that she only had one choice. She would not make Charlie go back to his own time, now that she knew the terrible thing that he would have to decide to confront. She would keep him here with her, if that was what he wanted.

But he would have to decide for himself, with no more help from the future. She would not sway him with information about Mary. He'd have to check his conscience and decide.

And if he eventually found out about Mary? What then?

She didn't know the answer to that. If Charlie stayed here in the twentieth century, would she be messing with some kind of cosmic force, a strand of history that she ought not to be touching?

13

<hr>

It was the only right decision. The only moral choice. But it left her with a sense of anxiety that came bubbling up from her toes into the pit of her stomach.

Why were the right decisions always the impossible ones?

Keeping Charlie in Greenleigh was going to cause her innumerable headaches. Preventing her mother from finding out didn't concern her too much. She didn't see her mother getting better anytime soon. Charlie was old enough to be a senior in high school—he wouldn't be around for long, she suspected. As soon as he got his feet firmly established in the twentieth century, she suspected he would zip off for parts unknown. Perhaps west, perhaps to the big city somewhere.

But school! She wasn't sure of how to engineer the permissions and forms. They would have to forge some paperwork. Maybe he could say he was eighteen, and bypass parents. Prior school records? Ha. There would be none of that. But what Charlie didn't know wouldn't hurt him. He wasn't looking for a diploma. He was looking for a way into the twentieth century. Maybe he would change his mind about going to school, even. He said he was willing to work while studying on the side. If he wanted to be a poet, did it even matter if he had a diploma? Wasn't it more important to read a lot of books and write a lot of poetry?

She wondered for a moment if he would let her read something he'd written. Or maybe—was there something already upstairs in the attic?

That old dustheap of junk. She had tried not to think about the wasteland that was the Burnham history, up there in the attic, but now she understood that a lot of the answers to her questions were to be found up there.

But first, there was one obvious task that she needed to execute before she committed to this crazy path before her.

Elisabeth replaced the book on Drew Clark and took Charlie with her up the stairs. She didn't want to subject him to the elevator again, but she had to get back upstairs to talk to Shawn. Maybe he could help them.

Charlie followed her in silence. Elisabeth knew this was not a normal state of being for him. He was a chatty, cheerful person, and his casual assumption that he could live in twentieth-century Greenleigh with no consequence to himself or the world of Linfield in 1895 stemmed from his native optimism and belief in himself. He wasn't wondering if Greenleigh would accept him, or if his family would suffer without him. He was self-reliant, and confident that he would produce excellent work no matter where he landed...just not in a factory in 1895.

But he had used the word "kin." And if he understood the meaning of "kin," he couldn't possibly be feeling joy at this moment. He had felt he couldn't remain in Linfield, but he hadn't wished for the destruction of the mill. He had assumed that no one would mind if he slipped out of the 19th century quietly, without a word. He felt replaceable.

None of us are replaceable, Charlie.

"Aren't you hungry, Charlie?" She opened the door leading

into the far side of the top floor, where they had left Charlie's books on a cart.

"Yeah," he said listlessly.

"We're going home. We'll get something to eat. And I'll make up a bed for you. You must be exhausted." Elisabeth tried not to think about the fact that she still had to write a research paper and then she had to go to school the next day. What would happen to Charlie while she was in school? She didn't want to take him without thinking of a plan, first. And could she really keep him away from Mum? What would Mum do if she found him?

She couldn't think about this now.

"Yeah."

"Don't worry," she said, although the words rang false in her ears. "Don't worry, Charlie. We'll figure this out."

He nodded but didn't seem very interested. She urged him to take some poetry books with him from his stack, but he shook his head, so she grabbed a couple along with the volumes Shawn had set aside for her and went to check them out from the self-check station.

As luck would have it, Shawn was there in front of her, methodically running his own pile of books through the scanner. She would have turned and fled, but she couldn't get to the self-check station on the other side of the floor without passing him, anyway. And then there was Mrs. Murphy's questioning to worry about. Better to just face him, she decided.

She walked up boldly behind him. She tried to sound nonchalant.

"Thanks for the books," she said.

Shawn didn't turn around, but she saw him tense up slightly.

"Sure," he said. He had finished putting his books through but was comparing his stack to the paper print-out.

"I thought you were doing calculus homework," she continued, hoping that she hadn't offended him earlier.

"Finished it. Just grabbing some biographies for my pleasure reading."

Pleasure reading, Elisabeth thought. Someone who had his life under sufficient control that he had time to read! Then the not-too-nice thought entered her head that he probably didn't have to work a part-time job to make ends meet. With effort, she dismissed the thought from her head.

"Are you leaving?" She kept her tone pleasant.

"Are you?" Shawn snapped back.

Startled, Elisabeth didn't know how to reply. Shawn turned around. He stared right at her, hazel eyes looking both serious and demanding.

"Are you planning on doing that paper at home?"

"I—uh—yes, I suppose I was," she stammered.

"I thought you were going to work on it here, but it looks like you're leaving."

"I—I changed my mind," she said. She couldn't remember if she'd said anything about where she was planning to work on the paper.

"What about that guy?"

"Uh—you mean Charlie?" That was a stupid response! Obviously, he meant Charlie!

Shawn didn't reply, merely waited.

Elisabeth turned to look behind her. Charlie had followed her over to the self-check station but hadn't seemed interested in twentieth-century book cataloguing technology. He'd wandered off to lean against the railing, his back facing them, looking down onto the main floor below. He was determined to avoid the elevator, it seemed, so he was waiting for her next to the stairs.

"Are you going to tell me who Charlie is?" Shawn said quietly.

Elisabeth turned around again. She felt herself flushing. What should she say?

"He's just a guy," she began, but Shawn stopped her.

"I'm not stupid, Beth. He's more than just a guy. I've never seen him before. And I've never seen you with anyone here at the library. I've seen you here for weeks. It took me forever to get up the courage to talk to you."

"To me?" Elisabeth felt the unholy urge to laugh hysterically. Shawn Waterstone was afraid to talk to *her* of all people? Elisabeth Burnham, who'd just been rejected from the National Honor Society?

"Yes, you!" Shawn snapped. "Don't laugh."

"I'm sorry. I'm not laughing at you. I'm laughing at—well, anyway," Elisabeth said in a rush. "Thank you. For talking to me." She stopped, feeling herself flush even redder. She was making a mess.

Shawn appeared not to listen. He went on, "Charlie doesn't go to our school, or I'd know who he was. And you hardly talk to anyone at school, anyway."

Elisabeth felt a growing sense of irritation. Was he keeping a notebook on her behaviors? Counting the number of people she sat with for lunch? Which, she thought angrily, was zero.

This was humiliating, and she didn't like being humiliated.

Clenching her jaw, she stepped forward to scan her books. Shawn moved aside, watching as she slid first one book, then the next across the glass.

There was silence for a moment as she completed the check-out process and pulled her receipt from the machine. She stacked up the books, then lifted her chin and met Shawn's gaze.

He was still waiting for his answer.

This was too much. Shawn didn't have any right to monitor

her movements. And it bothered her that he seemed to think she was friendless and therefore desperate for company.

All right, that wasn't fair, she admitted to herself. Shawn could date anyone he wanted. He didn't need to scheme to grab a date with someone who was one of the more friendless members of the sophomore class. He didn't need to scheme at all. She was being oversensitive and proud.

She opened her mouth to apologize, but then changed her mind. Instead, she said, "Do you have a car?" She knew he had a car but couldn't think of a way to bring up the subject.

Shawn blinked in surprise. "A car? Yeah, I have a car."

"Can you give us a lift?"

"Sure." Shawn looked perplexed. He rubbed the back of his head with one hand, then looked down the corridor where Charlie was still leaning against the railing, gazing down at the main floor of the library. The librarians were dimming the lights.

"Charlie, too," Elisabeth added, to make sure he understood that she wasn't asking for a date.

"Yeah, of course. Home?"

"No." Elisabeth paused, trying to think through the fuzzy haze of a plan in her head. She didn't know what she was trying to do, exactly. She was just trying to push her way forward, through a fog of indecision, assorted facts on a warped timeline, and—

—at that moment, Charlie turned around as if to check to see where Elisabeth was, and in that brief second where his sad eyes held hers, she made her decision.

"Linfield," she said. "Could you take us to Linfield?"

14

Charlie perked right up when he saw Shawn following Elisabeth down the corridor.

"Hey," he said. He sounded almost excited. Shawn, in contrast, cast a wary eye at him before walking right past him and around the bend of the railing. He started to descend the stairs, then paused and looked up.

Charlie was waiting for Elisabeth, whispering at her. "Do I follow him?" he asked. "Are we going with him? He looks like he's leaving."

"Go ahead," Elisabeth murmured. She wasn't entirely sure if her plan made sense, but it was the only thing she could think of, and she needed to do something, anything, before carrying out a drastic plan—or lack of a plan—to keep Charlie in the twentieth century.

They descended the stairs together, hurrying to catch up to Shawn, whose long legs had already taken him into the lobby and out the door. Elisabeth gasped as she emerged from the relative warmth of the library into the frigid reality of a January night in Greenleigh. She fumbled with her scarf, trying to tuck it more securely into the neck of her coat, before reaching into her pockets for her hat and gloves. She glanced over at Charlie, who had hunched over in response to the wind.

"Where's your hat?" she asked. He'd been wearing it on the way to the library, but it was gone.

"Dunno. I guess I left it with the books? Oh, I know. I stuck it on a shelf. When I was sitting on the floor."

"Oh, Charlie," Elisabeth groaned in frustration.

Charlie waved away her concern. "It's all right. I'll survive." He was about to say more, but his speech faded as Shawn stopped in front of a beater of an old car and pulled out a ring of keys from his pocket.

"I say," he said in admiration. "Are we going to ride in one of these? Is this here your—" Charlie seemed to be at a loss for what to call the car, so Elisabeth interrupted him.

"It's a car, Charlie."

"A cart?"

"No, a car. We call them cars."

"That's just fizzing!"

"Fizzing?"

Charlie wasn't listening. He was walking around the car, touching it gently with his gloved fingers. Thank goodness he'd held onto the gloves, Elisabeth thought.

"All right, get in," Shawn grunted. He had put his books into the back seat and was moving his school backpack out of the front seat. Charlie stopped, looking uncertain. Elisabeth went over to open the door to the back seat for him, and he climbed in. She got into the front and shut the door. For a moment, they all sat quietly. Then Shawn inserted the key into the ignition and turned on the engine. Charlie jumped, then howled as an icy blast of air hit him in the face.

"Lord!" he screeched. Hastily, Shawn reached over to point the blower away.

"Sorry," he said, raising his voice above the sound of the fan.

"You'll have to wait a minute before it heats up. It really struggles in this weather."

"It's the heat, Charlie," Elisabeth explained. "Cars have heat in them."

Shawn looked at Elisabeth oddly. When she didn't elaborate, he said, "Where are we going?"

"First, we need to get food," she said. "We're starved. We've missed dinner. Can you take us to a drive-through?"

"Sure. Which one?"

"I don't know. I don't—I don't go to drive-throughs," she said.

"You said you wanted to go to Linfield," Shawn said. "There are some places on the way out of town, we'll hit one of those."

"Why are we going to Linfield?" Charlie asked. He'd been sitting quietly in the back seat, staring at the dashboard over Shawn's shoulder and intermittently holding his hands up in the now warming blast of air from the blowers. At the mention of Linfield, however, he put his hands down and leaned forward. Glancing up at the rearview mirror, Elisabeth saw his brow furrow. She turned around to find him frowning darkly.

"I don't like this plan. We should go back to your house, Beth. And look in the attic."

At this, Shawn turned around. "You know what? The two of you need to explain what's going on. Where do you live, Charlie? And why are you with Beth?"

Before she could silence him, Charlie replied, "We're cousins. And I'm from Linfield. And that's why Beth wants you to take us there. But I don't want to go to Linfield. I'm staying at Beth's and it's late." He glared at Elisabeth.

Shawn's suspicious gaze went from Charlie to Elisabeth. She felt her courage flagging, but said, "Can we get food? And I'll explain. Please, Shawn?"

Reluctantly, he turned again and put the car into drive. As he pulled out of the parking space in front of the library, Charlie sat back in his seat. Elisabeth glanced up at the rearview mirror, where she could see his amazed expression until he scooted to the driver's side so he could gaze out the window.

"We're going so fast!" he exclaimed as Shawn made a right turn and accelerated as he cruised down the main Greenleigh drag. At this hour, no shops were open, and it was far too cold for the few restaurant-goers to stroll on the streets after dinner.

"Yeah, only crazy people go out on a night like this," Shawn muttered. He glanced at Elisabeth, who flushed.

"Thank you for doing this, Shawn," she said meekly. "And I'm starving. I know this wasn't the dinner out that you planned. But I would have said yes if I could have." She nodded toward Charlie.

Shawn's expression softened, and he nodded. For a few minutes, they were silent, as he navigated the empty town streets leading to the state highway. Soon, they were pulling into a burger drive-through.

Elisabeth suddenly remembered that she needed money. Panicking, she checked her wallet, but she had skipped lunch that day so she still had the five-dollar bill for the week. She handed it to Shawn, but he waved it away.

"Let me," he said briefly. "It was supposed to be a date, anyway."

Charlie was gazing in confusion at the menu. He jumped when the speaker crackled. Shawn leaned out to order burgers, fries, and shakes, then rolled up the window in a hurry.

"Man!" he complained. "It's crazy cold out."

"That was a menu," Charlie said. "But it had a voice?"

Shawn glanced at Elisabeth.

"Charlie's never been through one of these. Actually, I don't know the last time I've been through one, either. We don't have a car—anymore," she finished.

Shawn nodded and turned back to the window. "I know. I'm

sorry. And I'm sorry about this, too." He waved a hand at the window. "I wanted to take you somewhere decent. Not a drive-through."

"Hey. It's okay," Elisabeth said. "This is a treat. I don't do this often. So it's special."

"I don't understand about the voice," Charlie persisted.

"Charlie, it's wireless. That's all. You know, like—like a—" When was the radio invented, Elisabeth asked herself. She felt as if she'd learned that fact at some point but couldn't bring it to mind. Had it existed in 1895?

"The wireless was probably invented in about 1895," Shawn said absently. "Guglielmo Marconi. An Italian inventor."

Elisabeth turned around. She exchanged glances with Charlie and shook her head slightly. He looked chastened and nodded reluctantly.

Shawn rolled down the window to take the bag of food. He handed it to Elisabeth so he could dig his wallet out of his pocket. Steam wafted up out of the bag, and for a moment, Elisabeth shut her eyes, breathing in the hot-oil scent of hot French fries. She couldn't remember the last time she'd had a real French fry. Meals at home were frequently pasta and jar sauce nowadays.

Shawn rolled the window up hastily, muttering, "Wicked cold!" He pulled the car over to a nearby parking space. Elisabeth was already handing food back to Charlie, who knew exactly what to do with it. He tore the wrapping off and began wolfing it down.

Elisabeth leaned forward to turn on the radio. It was tuned to a nighttime jazz show on public radio. Charlie stopped eating for a moment, his eyes wide, then seemed to decide that it wasn't worth asking questions if it meant he couldn't eat at the same time. He went back to his food, leaning back to stare through the window as he munched.

"I promised to tell you what was going on," she began, trying to keep her voice low and under the sound of the music.

Shawn turned the volume up on the rear speakers before replying. "You know what, Beth. I guess I don't really care. If Charlie's your cousin—"

"I think he's my cousin," Elisabeth said. She couldn't be completely honest, but she felt she needed to tell him what truth she could. "He was hanging around the woodshed at home. I know I'm related to the Davises. We've got Davis stuff kicking around in our attic. Pictures and memorabilia. I know he's part of the family. And we bumped into Mrs. Miller on the way to the library. When Charlie said his name, she seemed to take it in stride that he was a relation."

At this, Shawn rolled his eyes. Everyone knew Mrs. Miller.

"But you don't know each other," he said.

"Right. We've never met. All I know is he's from Linfield."

"He's run away from home, then."

"Probably. I'm just trying to figure him out. I'm sorry—this all sounds weird, I know. But he wants to live with us—"

Shawn choked on his shake. "What?"

"—and I just don't know what's going on," Elisabeth finished. That seemed to be about the best she could do in terms of skirting the truth, she decided. She'd let Shawn fill in the gaps in his own mind.

"So you're trying to take him home?"

"Sort of. He doesn't want to go home."

"I'm not going home," Charlie announced from the back seat. He had wolfed down his burger and fries, and was sucking happily at the thick milkshake through a straw that was obviously too narrow for it.

Elisabeth and Shawn exchanged looks. Shawn crumpled the wrapper for his burger into a ball and tossed it into the food bag. "All right. I get it. Or I think I do. Charlie," he said, turning around in his seat. "We're going to iron this out. All right?" His voice had taken on a brotherly tone, as if he were talking to a not-very-bright toddler.

"I don't want to go home," Charlie repeated. "If the mill's burned down, there's no point to being there, anyway."

"What mill?" Shawn asked.

Elisabeth shook her head at him, but Charlie said, "The mill. The Linfield sawmill."

Shawn's brow cleared. "Oh, that mill? I know where that is. What do you mean by burned down?"

This time, Elisabeth reached out a hand in spite of herself. She clutched at Shawn's leg, covered with his heavy parka, and gripped at it in a warning gesture. Startled, Shawn looked at her, and she shook her head again.

"We saw it—in this book of pictures. It was burned to the ground," Charlie continued.

"Shawn, can we go? See the mill? Charlie, you don't mind that, do you?"

Charlie shook his head. "Naw. I can take it. It'll be sad—and strange. But I can take it."

Elisabeth gripped Shawn's leg again. This time, he put his hand on hers. His eyes met hers, and she would have pulled her hand away in embarrassment except that she needed him to understand—she needed him to stop questioning Charlie and to just take them to Linfield.

However, the expression in his eyes was far from offended. He believed in her, she thought. He believed in her and wanted to help.

"Sure," he said slowly. He squeezed her hand. "Sure, I'll take you."

15

———

Shawn didn't take them via the interstate, but chose the forty-mile-an-hour state highway that ran due west out of Greenleigh. They passed long stretches of frozen cornfields with last autumn's debris still cluttering the ground and dark woods hanging over tumble-down stone walls. There were no streetlights—who would need streetlights on a country road between two small New England towns?

Charlie had his nose to the window, occasionally yelping aloud at the speed of the car. Shawn appeared to have decided that Charlie's odd remarks weren't worth thinking about. Elisabeth hoped he'd accepted her half-truth about Charlie. She hadn't exactly lied. She'd just left out the detail about time travel.

What did she hope to find in Linfield? She didn't know. But she had a gut instinct about Charlie. She would help him stay, but she wanted to establish what he was fleeing. If they could see the mill, the concrete, 3-D representation of everything he wanted to leave behind—maybe it would bring some clarity to his purpose. Maybe she would feel less jittery about helping him to avoid his fate.

Maybe this wasn't about Charlie. Maybe this was about her.

She toyed with a paper napkin in her hands, smoothing it and folding it over and over again.

Maybe she was the one who needed to know what Charlie's history would have been. Maybe she was the one who needed to see the mill with her own eyes. Maybe, in typical Elisabeth Burnham fashion, she needed to do enough research to come to her own conclusions before she made any decisions.

All she knew was that she would only know what she was doing when she was doing it.

"You're going to be up late with that paper," Shawn commented.

Elisabeth gave a start. She hadn't thought about the paper since she'd put her stack of research material through the self-check machine.

How stupid, to have to do a dumb paper that even the teacher didn't want to read—when Charlie's life hung in the balance. And not just Charlie's life. But perhaps her own. Because she might find out something about the Burnhams, she thought. Dad hadn't said much about the Davises. And neither had Grampy, although both of them seemed to prize those old books and albums up in the attic. They'd gotten shoved into boxes by Mum, who thought they attracted bugs. But Daddy had loved the old attic treasures. He used to take Elisabeth up with him and help her set up the old dollhouse, then let her play as he browsed through the old books and photo albums.

To her surprise, she felt a lump in her throat, painful and hard.

Poor Daddy, she thought. For him, life sucked. And whenever he became overwhelmed by his life as a grown-up, he dove back into the attic to try to figure himself out.

And he'd never quite managed it. He'd been cut off from the rest of life too soon.

But then there was Mum. Mum hadn't been happy for as long as Elisabeth could remember. There were photos lying about that suggested that she had been happy with Daddy once. But those frozen moments of time were not in Elisabeth's memory. They were captured moments, printed on paper, not experienced. She couldn't even conjure up an image in her mind of Mum laughing happily. What would that even sound like? It seemed impossible that she had once been young and optimistic. That she had looked forward to a happy life with James Burnham. That she had willingly ditched the advice of her Vermont family when they warned her that James Burnham would not be a solid provider or companion.

What was real, then? The photos of a laughing young woman? Or the sad shell of a person who spent all her time in her room?

Could they both be real?

What was reality, anyway? Was the photo of the burned-out shell of the mill reality? How about the flesh-and-blood Charlie in the back seat of Shawn's car? Was memory real? Or was reality based in only the here and now?

Linfield town center was not far from Greenleigh center, about a half-hour drive, and since the drive-through was already on the edge of town, it only took them fifteen minutes to arrive at the Linfield Mill. The mill was on an industrial road leading out of town center, on the banks of the river that had powered it for a hundred years before electricity transformed it. A disused rail line passed through the mill property, and as Shawn slowed the car down and prepared to park, they bumped over tracks that had once seen busy traffic throughout western New England and upstate New York, all the way up to Montreal, but were now weedy and unkempt.

Elisabeth turned around in her seat as Shawn cursed the raised curb of the mill's rear lot. He'd been unable to see it in the dark and had scraped the undercarriage of his car. Charlie was staring hard out the window, his eyes fixed on the red brick buildings, the loading dock with a dozen bays, and the wide asphalt parking lot, empty under the glare of enormous lights.

"That's the mill," he said softly. "It looks the same, but different."

"Hoping the town cops don't hang out here and drink coffee during the night shift," Shawn said. "We're trespassing."

"I don't see anyone," Elisabeth said.

"They've got to have some kind of security system."

"Maybe a guard? We should be careful," Elisabeth agreed. "But can we drive up closer? This is the back. I'd like to see the front, the street side."

"Sure," Shawn agreed. "This is where we always come to pick up orders, but I guess I can figure out where the front entrance is." He continued down the street and around the block to the other side. There was no one on the street—not even a parked car—which made sense on a frigid January night. There was another parking lot across the street from the main entrance, presumably for customers who were headed for the business offices rather than to handle lumber orders.

"It's too cold to park in the lot and walk," Shawn commented. "I'm going to just pull into that handicapped parking space right on the street, in front of the main entrance. I hope they don't have a guard in that vestibule, or we're going to get questioned." He swung around, doing a U-turn in the street, in order to pull up right in front of the entrance. There were multiple doors and windows all along a series of connected red brick buildings, but there was a sturdy sign made of black metal in front of one of the doors. It read, LINFIELD MILL, in gold lettering, with EST 1823 in smaller gold letters underneath.

"Wow, 1823," Shawn muttered. Elisabeth remembered that he was an American history aficionado. Pity she couldn't just do a presentation for her history class instead of a paper, because she was doing a deep dive into New England economic history right then and there.

"There used to be a wood frame building here," Charlie said. "But that was before my time. My father tore it down. It was a firetrap." He looked at Elisabeth. "We had a huge brick building. But not like these. These are new."

Shawn looked perplexed. He turned to Elisabeth, about to say something, but Charlie was fussing with the door, so he turned off the engine and got out of the car. Elisabeth hastily followed, but Shawn got to Charlie before she did. He opened the door, and Charlie emerged.

For a moment, he didn't leave the side of the car. He gazed at the building from where he stood, craning his neck to look up above them, from one end of the building complex to the other.

"Lord," Elisabeth heard him mutter.

After several moments, he breathed a deep, whooshing sigh. She saw his breath in a cloud of mist and reached out to put her hand on his arm.

"Are you all right?" she asked quietly.

"These are new," he repeated. He paused, then added, "It's beautiful. So clean and new."

"We've gotten lumber here," Shawn said. "Both for the factory and for home."

"I wonder if there are still Davises here," Charlie said.

Shawn gave Elisabeth a sharp look, which she chose to ignore. She was going to have to take her position, she knew. It was time for her to decide—help Charlie or not.

She was going to help him.

"Charlie," she said. "Charlie, I'll help you stay. I don't know what that means—yet—but we'll work it through."

He didn't look at her but continued to gaze upwards at the several stories of tall windows, all of them pristine.

"You see, everything is okay. They've rebuilt the mill."

Charlie still said nothing.

Elisabeth stepped backwards slightly, attempting to take in the view better. It was a long series of buildings, so she had to sweep her gaze from left to right and strain her eyes to see to the end of the street on both sides. As she did so, she thought she saw something gleaming to her right. She walked toward it, and as she did so, she realized that she was seeing a smooth marble plaque of considerable size and heft, placed squarely between the main entrance and what appeared to be an employees' entrance immediately to the right. There was a powerful light nestled in a decorative grove of rhododendron bushes planted around the employees' entrance, trained directly onto the plaque.

She stopped in front of it.

LINFIELD MILL

DEDICATED 1908

TO MARY ELISABETH DAVIS, OWNER

WHO BROUGHT US THROUGH THE FIRE

"Charlie!" she called. "Come look at this."

Shawn hurried over. Charlie followed more slowly.

"Who's Mary Elisabeth Davis?" Shawn asked.

"Kin," Elisabeth replied, before Charlie could answer.

"Mary Elisabeth took over the mill," Charlie said. "Then—"

"Don't," Elisabeth warned. "Don't leap to any conclusions. You don't know why or how this happened. Only that it did, and the people were grateful. And she built this." She pointed at the building. "The workers erected this monument ten years after the fire."

"My name's not there," Charlie said. He turned to Elisabeth.

His face was solemn. "Maybe I never went back. Or maybe I died."

"Does it matter?" Elisabeth pleaded. "You have this chance right now to follow your heart. And you aren't hurting anyone by doing it."

Charlie nodded once, then twice. "Yes. Yes, you're right." Then he smiled slightly. "Mary Elisabeth was a smart girl. She would've been a better boss than me of all those men."

Elisabeth smiled back, but she felt her stomach tense. There was that side to the Mary Elisabeth story that she hadn't told Charlie, but she wasn't going to tell him. Not now, at any rate. He needed to decide without letting the future interfere. And a seventeen-year-old boy didn't need to process an ugly tale of domestic violence and addiction.

The plaque was on the left side of the employee entrance. Elisabeth realized that there were lights on both sides of the entrance, and Charlie must have come to the same conclusion at the same moment, because both of them started to walk over to the other side of the entrance at the same time. Then they saw the second plaque.

Before Elisabeth could move, Charlie hurried forward. He pushed the branches of an ice-encrusted rhododendron bush out of the way and leaned in to examine the plaque. Whereas the plaque dedicated to Mary was gray marble with plain black lettering, this one was light brown with gold lettering.

"What does it say?" Elisabeth exclaimed. When Charlie did not reply, she pushed him aside impatiently.

A TRIBUTE

TO MY BELOVED BROTHER CHARLIE
HIS COURAGE AND LOVE
MARY ELISABETH DAVIS, 1899

She stood, mouth agape. What did it mean?

A "tribute" wasn't a "memorial." So Charlie wasn't dead...she hoped.

Or was she just obsessing on the meaning of the word, to no purpose?

Had Charlie survived?

If Charlie were thriving at the mill, working alongside his sister, why wouldn't his name have been on the plaque from the workers?

And why would his sister have felt compelled to dedicate a separate monument to her brother if he were alive and well?

Charlie stepped back. The branches of the rhododendron snapped into place, showering icy crystals of old snowfall onto the ground.

His face had no expression that she could see in the glow of the bright light trained on the plaque. But when he turned to face her, she could see that he had made up his mind. His jaw was set, his eyes bright.

"Charlie?" she asked tentatively.

"We don't know what it means," he said. His voice was firm. "Except that it's safe for me to not go back. I'm not part of the mill anymore after the fire." He pushed his way past Elisabeth.

"Are we good?"

It was Shawn, still standing next to the first plaque.

Startled, Elisabeth turned to him. She had forgotten that she was supposed to keep Shawn out of the time travel part of the story, and she and Charlie had lapsed into speaking frankly. Did he think she was crazy? He hadn't seen the second plaque, however, and he made no move to see what they had been looking at.

"I'm freezing," Shawn continued. He was stamping his feet, moving from side to side. "It's got to be single digits, maybe even zero. I'm going to the car to make sure I can start it." He turned and hurried toward the car.

He hadn't asked any questions, and his expression gave nothing away. Maybe he hadn't heard them.

Charlie said the words for her. "Do you think he knows what we're talking about?"

She shook her head. "No. I don't know."

"He's a good guy."

Elisabeth sighed. "Yes. He is." And she'd surely ruined any chance that they would ever go on that postponed dinner date. But she'd decided that kin mattered.

"Come on, Charlie. Let's go home."

———

16

When they got into the car, Shawn was fussing with the heat.

"Sometimes it works better with the air conditioning on," he said to no one in particular. "I'm just glad the car started. I'm going to park in the garage tonight instead of in front of the kitchen door. Even an extra five degrees will help get this old thing started tomorrow before school."

Elisabeth smiled sadly. She would be walking to school in the cold, as per usual. Without Charlie, however. She would need to figure out how to get him into school without creating a lot of drama, and for that she would need at least a day or two.

She would have to warn him about her mother's habits so they didn't come across each other during the day while she was gone. He'd have to avoid going upstairs, and he'd have to stay out of the kitchen just in case she got hungry and came downstairs, which she usually did at around one in the afternoon. And he'd have to avoid clanging about with the wood stove or the sink. And not answer the door. And—

She sighed heavily, forgetting where she was for a moment.

"Why don't I pick you up tomorrow?" Shawn said.

She started.

"What?"

"I said, why don't I pick you up before school tomorrow? It's too cold to walk. I assume you walk? You live too close for the bus."

Elisabeth was too stunned to reply. Shawn wanted to take her to school? But—

"You two sound like you're courting," came Charlie's voice from the back seat. He sounded faintly amused.

"We are," Shawn said indifferently. "So don't interfere."

"Oho," Charlie chortled. "No, sir."

"And it's just too damn cold." Shawn leaned forward to fuss with the blower again, his gloved fingers slipping as he tried to manipulate the vent. The car was still not warm, despite the fact that they had been driving for ten minutes and were nearly in Greenleigh center.

"Let me," Elisabeth said. "You watch the road." She removed her right glove and attempted to turn the vent toward Shawn. It finally unstuck itself with a loud click. "Better?"

"A little," he said.

"And about tomorrow," she began.

"I'll be by at 7:30." She could tell from his tone that he was becoming irritable, probably from cold and fatigue. She decided that it was fortunate that he wasn't pressing Charlie with questions. Shawn Waterstone taking her to school would cause a huge uproar, especially in first-period American history class, and she had thought to point that out, but decided to err in favor of keeping him distracted from questioning her about Charlie.

"Thanks," she said.

She suddenly realized that they were on Main Street.

"Let me tell you where I live," she said.

Shawn laughed. "Do you think I don't know where you live?"

Elisabeth blinked. "How would you know where I live?"

"Everyone knows where you live. The other people on that street are a hundred years old. You're the only young person in that group of houses. Church Street, right?" Shawn was slowing down the car.

"Shawn," Elisabeth blurted, "can you drop us off before the house?" She was afraid Mum would be looking out the front hall window, if she happened to be up.

"Sure. It's cold, though. Don't you want to avoid the walk?"

Elisabeth ran through a list of plausible lies in her mind, then decided not to bother. She was going to be straight with him.

"My mum doesn't know about Charlie," she said. "I'm afraid if she finds out, she'll freak. She's—not well, you know? She hasn't been herself since my dad died."

"Beth," Shawn said. He was pulling over to the curb across the street, behind an enormous tree, and cut the headlights. No one could see them, not even nosy old Mrs. McPherson next door. He turned to her. "Beth, that was two years ago? Am I right? Your dad's accident? So your mom's been sick for two years?"

Elisabeth nodded. No one except the church ladies and the librarians ever asked about her mom. She had never had a conversation about her home life with a school mate.

"Do you have help?"

"No—but we're fine," she said. "The church ladies keep an eye on us."

"Church ladies?"

"From the Congregational church. You know, I live on Church Street? So, you know—the church?" She tried to joke.

Shawn didn't look convinced, but he held his tongue. "I'll pick you up tomorrow at 7:30. Go work on that paper." He turned in his seat. "Charlie, you're lucky you found Beth."

"She found me, actually," Charlie replied. "But yeah, I know. I'm lucky."

"I'll see you tomorrow, probably."

"Thank you, Shawn." Charlie ducked his head shyly.

For not asking more questions, Elisabeth thought. Then, realizing that Charlie would need someone to open the door for him, she gathered up her things to leave. As she reached for her purse and her books, Shawn caught her hand in his briefly and gave it a squeeze without looking at her. She paused, then smiled and gently pulled her hand away.

"See you tomorrow," she said.

She and Charlie crossed the street quickly, then walked the block over to the Burnham house. Elisabeth gave Charlie a warning look and put her finger to her lips as they tiptoed up the front steps. He nodded. She shook the doorknob as she opened the door, then shut it with a loud thud. Her noisy entrance gave Charlie the opportunity to dart through the darkened hallway and into the kitchen beyond. There was a single dirty dish in the sink, and a half-full glass of water to the side. Otherwise, the kitchen looked just as it had when they'd left for the library.

"Mum?" Elisabeth called quietly. There was no answer. She stood in the front hall, listening, but the house was silent.

Probably asleep, she thought. She began to remove her scarf, hat, and gloves.

Charlie was helping himself to a glass of water. He looked so comfortable, standing at the kitchen sink, that Elisabeth was forced to remember that he had practically grown up in this house himself, just as she had.

She shoved the wad of knitwear into the sleeve of her coat and hung it up on the coat rack, then went in to join him, slinging her books on the kitchen table. Charlie held up his glass to offer her some water, but Elisabeth pulled out the makings of tea from the cupboard above the sink.

"I'm cold. And I'll need the caffeine to do this stupid paper," she muttered.

"What's 'caffeine'?" Charlie responded.

"It's the stuff in tea and coffee that keeps you awake." Elisabeth put the water on the stove to boil. Charlie watched, fascinated, as she turned on the gas burner.

"That's new," he commented.

Elisabeth laughed. "Not really. Just new to you. You'll get used to it. But this stove has got to be fifty years old, at least."

Charlie plunked himself down in a chair. "Aunt Elisabeth always had the latest of everything. They were rich."

"Richer than you? Than the Davises?"

"Yeah. I think so."

"Maybe they just spent more money on beautiful things like books. You had to be pretty comfortable, owning a sawmill."

Charlie shrugged. "I think it cost a lot of money to run that place. Aunt Elisabeth always bought us a lot of presents, I figured it was because all of Father's money went back into the mill to keep it going." He paused, then said hesitantly, "You don't think I'm a bad person for not going back, do you?"

"Of course not," Elisabeth responded. Little bubbles were pinging in the kettle, so she put a tea bag in a cup for herself. Charlie shook his head when she offered him a cup.

"The mill looked—good. I thought it might have looked like that picture. Ruined."

"Shawn says his family gets lumber from Linfield. It sounds like the mill's business is doing fine."

"What does Shawn's family do?"

"I'm not sure," Elisabeth admitted. "They have a factory. I think it's wool or yarn or something like that."

"Then he's going to run it?"

"No," Elisabeth said. "He's going to college next year. Harvard."

"Why? Who's going to run the factory, then? Does he have a brother? Or—a sister?"

"No, he's an only child."

"Then who's going to run the factory?" Charlie repeated. He sounded baffled.

Elisabeth shrugged. The pinging had turned into a steady hiss of bubbling, so she turned the burner off and poured the water into her cup. It wasn't quite boiling, but that was okay for tea. She went to join Charlie at the table.

"Who knows? But he's too smart not to go to college. Maybe he'll come home afterwards and run the factory. Or maybe not. Things are different now, Charlie. We have more choices, and kids don't listen to their parents like they used to."

"Huh. And this is a good thing? A modern thing?"

Elisabeth shook her head. "I don't really know. What do you think?"

Charlie put his head down on the table, his cheek against the surface. His eyes drooped. "I don't know," he said finally. "All I know is that I don't want to run a sawmill. But now, because of that plaque, I know that Mary Elisabeth is going to run it. And the second plaque makes it clear that I had nothing to do with the place." He paused. Then he continued, "I keep wondering what I did, where I went, why I wasn't the one to run it. But I don't know if I like how it feels—that I left Mary Elisabeth behind with such a big job."

Charlie's words hovered in the air, as Elisabeth wrestled with his unspoken fear. Had he died in that fire?

Mary Elisabeth was a strong person, she thought.

"But how do you know she didn't like it? Maybe she actively wanted to run the factory?"

"Not Mary Elisabeth," Charlie said, closing his eyes now.

"She hated the rough environment of the sawmill just as much as I did. She was so romantic. She wanted to be a lady, with fine clothes and plenty of books. She wanted to run a book club like Aunt Elisabeth did and go to the theater. I can't see her running that mill. I guess that's what feels so strange. I never thought if I left, it would fall to her to take care of the mill. Puts a new spin on things."

"Charlie," Elisabeth said gently. "You're tired. Let me fix you up a room. There are rooms in the back of the parlor that Mum never goes into. It'll be cold at first because we don't heat them, but if we leave the parlor door open, it'll warm up enough for you. Let's get the parlor wood stove lit. Mum won't notice if we warm it up in there. And tomorrow we'll figure everything out."

"That sounds good," Charlie said. He lifted his head. "I'll do the wood stove. You can't light a stove for nothin'."

"I beg your pardon?" Elisabeth retorted hotly, but decided the argument wasn't worth it. While Charlie lit the parlor wood stove, she opened the door to the closest small bedroom and found it frigid. She left the door open while she got another down comforter from the room next door and plunked it down on the bed.

"The tops of these comforters are dusty. I'm sorry about that. No one ever goes into these rooms. They're just guest bedrooms, and we never have guests."

"I used to stay in those rooms," Charlie said, leaning over to blow on the logs. "They look almost the same as they did back then."

"I keep forgetting that you grew up in this house, too, Charlie."

"Yeah. I was always so happy here."

"I hope you're still happy here," Elisabeth said. "We can make this work. I promise. Even if school doesn't quite work out —there are lots of ways for you to study and write."

"I know," Charlie said, rising. He dusted his hands. "I wanted this more than anything, and I badgered you into it. And now I'm kind of scared." He stood for a moment, looking around the parlor, still filled with all the old furniture of Elisabeth's youth. It was a room that didn't see much use, since Elisabeth played the piano only rarely, and Mum never played at all anymore. The antique sofa and rocker had beautiful upholstery, but they were threadbare. The braided rug was dusty and faded.

"Oh, Charlie." Elisabeth looked around at the room, wondering what he saw. She saw the remnants of better times, ignored and allowed to lapse into a dust heap of time. It wasn't fair to Charlie, she knew. He deserved a gleaming, bright, shiny future.

Mum does, too, she thought. *And so do I.*

If "kin" means collapsing into disuse, it's bad.

"Elisabeth," Charlie said. He stepped toward her and held out his arms. "Thank you."

Surprised, she hugged him back. "Don't be so solemn," she begged. "We'll do this together. When you're famous, write me a poem."

"I will," he said, his voice muffled into her hair. "I swear I will."

"Now go to bed," she said, disentangling herself. She gave him a small push toward the bedroom. "I'm going to go up and peek in at Mum, to make sure she's asleep. She won't come downstairs tonight, and she never eats breakfast. I've got to do that paper. Go to bed. Things will look so much better tomorrow."

17

———

It was the clanking of the radiator in the front hall that woke her. One arm was stretched out, her cheek pressed against it, the metal coil of her spiral notebook pressing into the underside of her arm. She tasted hair in her mouth.

She'd fallen asleep over her homework. Slowly, Elisabeth raised her head, pulling strands of hair out of her face, blinking into the dim gray light of early morning.

The radiator clanked again, and she heard the groan of the boiler in the cellar as it rumbled under her feet. She was at the kitchen table, the light on, a cold cup of tea on the table beside her. Her eyes were sandy, her neck ached. Her notebook was filled with random, nonsensical squiggles trailing off the page where she'd tried to take notes but had dozed off. The stack of library books was in front of her, untouched.

Well. This isn't good, she thought.

This history paper was due today, and she hadn't written a thing. She wondered what happened when you didn't turn in something. She'd never done that before. And the paper was a big part of her grade. Which was exactly why Shawn kept nagging her about it.

Shawn!

Last night felt like a dream.

She leaned back in her chair, blinking her eyes into focus. She stretched, then winced. Her neck hurt, her back hurt, her butt hurt.

But wait. Something was odd.

She looked around the kitchen.

What was wrong here?

Everything seemed in place. It was still mostly dark outside but for the velvety gray tinge of morning. She squinted at the kitchen clock and saw that it was nearly seven.

She'd have to get ready if Shawn was picking her up for school. Wow. Was this really going to happen?

With a sinking feeling, she realized that he would ask her about the paper as soon as he saw her, and she would have to admit that she hadn't written it. She wondered if he wouldn't like her anymore once he'd decided that she was a disorganized mess who didn't always get her work done.

But that wasn't her normal self, she thought. It was just this once—because she was exhausted and worried about—

She suddenly realized what was wrong. The kitchen was warm. Not only was the kitchen warm, the entire *house* was warm.

But that made no sense! She could hear the boiler roaring its fury in the cellar, but she knew that the radiators were not the source of the warmth she was feeling. It had to be....

Elisabeth rose suddenly, nearly knocking her chair over behind her. She clutched at a sweater draped over her shoulders as it slid down her back. Bewildered, she pulled it off to look at it. This wasn't her sweater. It was a thick, scratchy, homemade wooly thing. It was oddly familiar, but it wasn't her sweater at all, definitely. She lifted it to her nose and sniffed tentatively. It smelled familiar, like—

—a musty drawer. From a closed room.

Charlie? Had Charlie put the sweater on her?

Elisabeth rushed over to the kitchen wood stove. Even before she reached it she knew that Charlie had been there. It was crackling, even with the damper open only a quarter of an inch. It wasn't smoking at all, and she could tell that the wood was burning slowly and evenly.

A terrible premonition swept over her. She turned to look at the table again, and this time she saw it.

The note. Written on a piece of brown paper bag, with a pencil.

She ran over and snatched it up.

Elisabeth—

As always, this house is magical. I've always loved it here. And when I lay down, it spoke to me.

I need to go home. Mary Elisabeth needs me. She's my sister, and she would never leave me behind. I can't abandon her.

But you and I, we're kin. So we'll never really be apart. Even though I'll miss having you right here with me.

I'll miss you less now that I've met Shawn. He's a good guy. I trust him to be kind to you.

Thank you for everything.

CHARLIE DAVIS

Elisabeth felt a sob catch at her throat. She hurried into the parlor where the wood stove was making cheerful crackling noises in its black pot belly. She could see that the door to the spare room she had opened up for Charlie was shut.

He was gone, then.

She couldn't believe it. She went to open the door, and

indeed, the room was empty, silent, both comforters folded neatly on the untouched bed.

Elisabeth let out a gasp as a thought entered her mind. Had he gone out to the shed? He might have frozen to death out there if he couldn't figure out how to get back to 1895.

She donned the scratchy old sweater, clearly a relic that Charlie had found in the spare room dresser, and went to pull on her outerwear. Fingers trembling, teeth chattering, she let herself out the back door and ran down the steps and across the lawn to the woodshed, her feet crunching along over the snow. She grasped at the shed door, lifted, tugged, and slid it open along its track.

The shed was empty, at first appearances. She heaved the door shut, then ventured inwards. She flicked on the light switch, recalling with wry amusement Charlie's startled reaction to the electric light.

The first thing she saw was the missing barrel of kindling, right in the middle of the floor, exactly where it had always been and should have been.

"Charlie?" she called.

Silence. She listened hard, unwinding her scarf slightly so she could hear even the faintest scuttling noises of critters under the piles of wood, and dry leaves and pine needles shifting in the draft. Slowly, she walked toward the woodpile where she had first seen Charlie—was that really only yesterday afternoon?— wondering if he had easily found the way back to 1895. The doorway to the past was probably behind the woodpile, in that space that he said he frequently hid behind.

She leaned over the top of the woodpile. But there was nothing. The floor was dry dirt. It was swept tidily, without even a footprint.

But wait—there was something. Next to the far wall, on top of the woodpile, she could see a dark object.

It was a book.

Charlie had been reading Mary Elisabeth's poetry book when she'd found him. He was worried that he'd lose it and get into trouble, she recalled. What a shame if he'd left it behind.

Elisabeth went to pick the book up. To her surprise, it was not the poetry book. It was a diary covered in handsome hand-tooled leather, soft and in a reddish-brown color. The initials MED were carved on the front.

Had Charlie forgotten to take this with him? But why had he been reading Mary Elisabeth's diary? Had he brought it with him from 1895? Had he found it somewhere in the house?

Suddenly, Elisabeth remembered. Charlie had disappeared on her when she was reckoning with Mum last night. He told her he'd been in the attic. He'd scolded her, in fact—because the attic was such a mess.

He had probably found the diary when he was up there.

Elisabeth was filled with a deep sense of foreboding. She removed her right-hand glove and opened the book.

The beginning pages were filled with youthful scrawls. There were notes on fashions, sketches of hats and shoes, complaints about this or that girl's fickle friendship. Elisabeth flipped through the pages impatiently.

Then she saw it. The first entry that started with, "Dietrich."

After that, nearly every page was about Dietrich. And before long, about Dietrich's love for her. And soon after that, about the fact that her parents would have a violent objection to the relationship, and then the plans for a secret elopement. "Escape from Linfield," she called it.

Elisabeth felt sick. She didn't want to keep reading. But she knew she had to find out what had made Charlie decide to go back home.

So she turned to the last entry. It had been marked with a clean, dry pine twig as a placeholder.

Charlie put this here for her, to make sure she read it.

At first, the date on the page confused her. It was long after the other diary entries. There had been a long pause between her plan to elope with Dietrich in 1895, and this last page. Strange. Hadn't Mary Elisabeth kept this diary with her? Why was it left at the Burnham home? Perhaps, Elisabeth thought, she didn't want anyone at home to discover it, and only wrote in it when she was visiting Aunt Elisabeth. She must have regarded the Burnham home as a safe space indeed, if she left her most private diary there rather than keeping it with her.

1897 June.

I am visiting Aunt Elisabeth today and have brought the two boys with me. Dietrich is asleep, having returned home in the wee hours of the morning after another night of gambling. I think he must have sold grandma's ruby ring this time, as I cannot find it. He has sold almost all of my jewelry. There is nothing left for him to take, and he'll be furious when he realizes this. I fear for my life, and for the boys' lives.

I am not going back. He does not take care of these boys. I do. I dare him to come and find me and to take them from me. Aunt Elisabeth knows all. Poor thing, she feels it is her fault I ran away with him. She will never forgive herself, I fear, for not watching me more closely when we visited. It is not her fault, it was never her fault. But she has fretted herself into a skeleton over it. I cannot continue to trouble her with my woes. I will return home to Mother and Father, and I will help with the mill in return for their charity. They will not be happy with me, but Aunt Elisabeth says she will talk to them. Surely they will not send me back to Dietrich. He will kill all three of us.

And poor, dear Charlie. He tried so hard to warn me, but we were already gone and married before he was found again that strange day in January. By the time he told me he knew what Dietrich was, it was too late. And I wouldn't listen, anyway. But he was right. I don't know how he knew so much about him, but he was right. Perhaps I can be of some help to him at the mill.

I will continue to keep this book of my most private thoughts in this attic hiding place at Aunt Elisabeth's. No one knows where it is, although sometimes I think Charlie has seen me put it away. He's a clever boy!

The men at the mill will protect me if Dietrich comes for us, I am sure of it. They are like kin to me, even with their rough ways.

Then written in smudged print right below:

I have read this and bear witness, a ghost of tomorrow. To Beth from Charlie

Charlie. He'd left this for her. And he had returned to rescue Mary Elisabeth from Dietrich.

But it hadn't worked. That much was clear. And even Charlie should have been able to figure that out, based on this last entry.

Elisabeth shuddered. She didn't know if she was physically cold, or perhaps psychologically wrecked, but she couldn't stop herself from shaking. Here was the rest of Charlie's story, right on this page. He'd returned on "that strange day in January," then discovered it was too late to stop Mary from marrying Dietrich. Elisabeth remembered the distant shouts for Charlie when she first discovered him in the shed. Charlie had said they were calling for him to go off and visit someone in North Adams, but they were actually searching for Mary. And she'd already run away.

Charlie went home to fulfill his destiny, which was to support Mary. Even knowing that he couldn't stop what was about to happen. Even with the question of whether he had survived the mill fire—with Mary's name on that plaque as the mill owner, it was entirely possible that he and his father had not made it through the fire, and that the mill had gone to Mary because of it.

Elisabeth put her glove back on with trembling fingers. She picked up the book and made her way to the door, hitting the light switch as she passed. As she pushed the shed door back into place, she thought about Mary. She'd heard parts of this story from her father, but they were the ghost-story parts having to do with the house across the street. All she knew from his tales was that Mary had taken the two boys and returned home to Linfield. Now that she knew that Mary had run the factory after the fire, she knew that Aunt Elisabeth had smoothed things over with the Davis parents, and that Mary had been all right.

But Charlie! What about Charlie? Had he survived the fire?

She had to know. She had to find out.

When Shawn pulled up in front of the house promptly at 7:30, Elisabeth was waiting. She ran down the steps to the car and waited for him to roll down the window.

"Did you get that paper done?" His voice was cheerful until he saw her face. "What happened? Is it Charlie?"

"Charlie's gone, Shawn." Elisabeth had calmed down. She managed to say the words without stammering.

"Gone? Gone where?" Shawn's brow wrinkled. "In this cold? How?"

Elisabeth shook her head. "Home," was all she could think of to say. Then she rushed on before he could respond. "I'm staying home today, Shawn. I'm sorry. I never finished that paper. And I have things I need to do at home. It's important."

"All right," Shawn said slowly. He gazed at her for a moment, then said, "I'll tell Mrs. Erdman you're not feeling well, that I saw you at the library last night. She'll probably let you turn the paper in late if you call the office and say you're sick. You should go. It's cold out."

"Thank you," she said. Then she leaned forward and kissed his cheek. "I miss him. I just need to know his story."

She turned around and ran into the house.

18

———————

Her mother asked vaguely whether she was going to school that day, but otherwise did not seem interested in the fact that she was at home. In fact, she was in better spirits today, getting dressed and coming downstairs for breakfast when Elisabeth called up the stairs.

"You don't usually eat breakfast, Beth," her mother said, picking up a knife to butter her toast.

"Neither do you, Mum," Elisabeth countered.

"I'm never hungry," her mother replied. She bit into the toast.

"I'm glad you're eating breakfast today," Elisabeth said. "I'm busy with a project for—for school. So I'm going to be up in the attic."

"The attic! Why on earth?" Her mother looked revolted. "What could you possibly need in the attic?"

"Old stuff. This is a history paper."

"Oh. Well. There's just old Burnham junk up there. Do as you please with it." A shadow crossed her mother's face. "Your father loved that stuff. I never understood it."

"I didn't, either."

"He used to take you up there."

"He did."

Elisabeth's mother was staring into space, holding her coffee cup in both hands. "What did you do up there?"

"Nothing at all. Played with the doll's house."

Her mother scoffed. "That old thing. It was broken from day one."

Elisabeth laughed. "Yeah. It was made of junk, essentially. I think a kid made it."

"I think I'm going to take a shower," her mother said, rising. "Thank you for breakfast, Beth." She carried her dishes to the sink. "Maybe I'll visit Mrs. McPherson next door. I'm feeling energetic today. And it's not as cold."

Elisabeth cast a sideways glance at the kitchen wood stove, which was still going strong. She'd put another log on the fire, but otherwise, Charlie's magic was still at work. The parlor was likewise still warm.

But the heat had not traveled up to the attic. At some point someone had put up a thick drape across the doorway, to block heat from escaping up there and to keep the rest of the house from being chilled. When Elisabeth pulled the drape aside, the cold in the attic stairwell momentarily took her breath away. But she'd come prepared, wrapped in the scratchy old sweater that Charlie had thought to drape over her when he'd found her asleep in the kitchen.

Thank you, Charlie, she thought.

She stood for a moment, looking around at the chaos of the attic, the clutter lying every which way. There were empty, broken suitcases and World War Two military footlockers, ancient rag rugs the color of mud after a hundred years of boots had ground dust into them, and wooden crates of books, dozens of them.

Where to start?

She didn't need to know everything, she thought. She just needed to know *something*.

She put her notebook and pencil down, then picked her way through the mess. The attic was enormous, the size of the entire footprint of the main part of the house. Where would Daddy have put that old family Bible? When he came up here, he tended to mess around with the old musical instruments and paintings, and not so much with the books. She was the one who'd found the poetry and novels that dated back to someone's old reading group at the turn of the century. But she didn't think the Bible would have ended up in that crate.

Well, she had to start somewhere. She went to the biggest crate of books and began to pull them out. It didn't take long for her to see that these were all novels, so she transferred her attention to the crate next to it. Again, these were more novels. A third one yielded more novels still.

Charlie was right, she thought. Aunt Elisabeth had a lot of books. It was no wonder that he was so happy in this house— and that he was so irritated at the mess in the attic. He must have been appalled to see how careless they were of the things that Aunt Elisabeth had prized so much.

She returned the books to their crates, annoyed. She looked around. It was going to take her forever to get through all of this stuff.

Her eye was caught by a piece of old furniture, a glass-fronted cabinet that looked as if it had seen better days. Some of the glass panes were missing, and she could see that on the bottom shelf, there was a single leather-covered book.

Aha! That was it. That made sense—the last time someone had looked through the Bible, they wouldn't have returned it to a box. It would have had a place of prominence, like in a cabinet or on a shelf.

She went to get it and sat down on the rough carpet next to the cabinet.

She'd seen this Bible many years before, and there had been some mention of the Davis family in it. She hoped that this would unlock the mystery of how she and Charlie were related.

It opened right at the page with the family record, right between the Old and New Testaments. There was a page of births, a page of marriages, and a page of deaths.

Elisabeth ran her finger quickly down the column of names on the marriage page and found what she was looking for. Aunt Elisabeth's name was inscribed next to the date 1875. Her maiden name had been Miller—a relation of old Mrs. Miller, she wondered?—and two generations before that was a Sarah Davis.

But so what? Elisabeth wondered. This is only a confirmation of what she already knew, that the Davises were cousins. Charlie wouldn't be in this Bible, of course.

Just as she was closing the pages of the Bible, she had a thought.

For a moment, she sat with the Bible in her lap, blinking. Then she flipped the book open again.

On the births page, there was an insertion written in small, neat letters. Elisabeth stood up and walked over to a nearby window so she could hold the book up to the light. The letters were tiny, written in beautiful cursive with what must have been an extremely well-sharpened pen.

"ANDREW CHARLES BURNHAM, 1899. By adoption."

She looked up, feeling a hollow in her chest where the breath was coming too quickly.

Charlie. It had to be. And 1899 was after the fire.

Charlie had survived the fire! At least, she hoped he had. Did these pieces fit together? She had to be sure.

Slowly, Elisabeth turned to the deaths page. There was a long list of deaths, ending with her grandfather's. Her father's death was missing, of course—Mum wouldn't have bothered with the Burnham family Bible. But Elisabeth wasn't looking for her father's name.

Her heart pounded. "Please, please, please," she muttered under her breath.

She found it.

Andrew Charles Burnham

Born 1877.

Died—

Her breath caught in her throat.

—1967.

She sank down, put her head in her hands. Her legs felt weak.

He hadn't died in the fire after all.

He'd lived a long life.

And what's more—he was her great-grandfather. Aunt Elisabeth had adopted him a few years after he returned from his overnight adventure in the twentieth century, and Mary had returned to the mill. Perhaps she still felt responsible for Mary's ill-fated liaison with Dietrich Behr. Or perhaps Aunt Elisabeth had taken it upon herself to give Charlie a different life.

But what had Charlie done after that point? Elisabeth cursed herself for not asking to hear more stories about the Burnhams. She remembered Grampy only dimly, and she hadn't been born when his dad—Charlie—had died. And the only way to learn more about Charlie would have been through Grampy.

Then she flipped back to the page of marriages. In 1905, Andrew Charles Burnham married Margaret Foster. From the look of the birth record, they'd had five children—the eldest named Elisabeth.

Elisabeth almost laughed out loud. That would be the Elisabeth who'd written the Drew Clark book, most likely! And that would have been Daddy's own Aunt Elisabeth. Another full circle.

She rose shakily, steadying herself with one hand against a dusty old bookcase containing a series of scrapbooks. Scrapbooks! Drew Clark's biographer, Elisabeth, was a photography expert, she thought. Were there photographs in these scrapbooks?

She put down the Bible carefully on one of the shelves, resolving to take better care of the old records in this attic. She chose one album randomly and opened it to a page in the middle.

These were family photographs, mostly posed in a studio. But as she leafed through the book, she came across the same photograph that she had seen at the library—a group of nattily dressed young people standing next to the theater building in Greenleigh. It was a better quality photograph than the one reproduced in the book, however, and she could see that the smudged face that had reminded her of Charlie was indeed Charlie Davis. The confident young woman next to him must have been his sister, Mary.

The photograph had become unglued from the page. Elisabeth picked it up and turned it over. There was a penciled note on the back.

"Charlie and Mary at the theater, ca 1900. No crutches!"

Crutches? Elisabeth wondered what that was about. She turned to the previous page, then to the page before that. There were photos of the burned-out hulk of the mill, as well as photos of the rebuilding. In one photo, Mary was posing with two boys in front of what was to become the new mill façade. Elisabeth wondered if they were her stepsons by Dietrich. Charlie stood a little way apart, leaning heavily on crutches. But he was smiling broadly at something or someone beyond the lens of the camera. Smirking, actually.

"Charlie," she said aloud. "You look like you've pulled one over on everyone. Even with those crutches." He must have been injured in the fire, she thought, but it didn't seem to be holding him back.

She put the book back on the shelf and pulled out another one. This one contained more studio portraits. This time she found Charlie and his wife, Margaret, and their children. These were taken years after the factory photograph with Mary. Life seemed to have gotten better after marriage.

As she turned the pages, a yellowed newspaper clipping fell out. It was so old that it seemed about ready to crumble in her hands as she picked it up.

It was a 1905 article from a Boston newspaper about the Linfield Mill and its lady owner, Mary Elisabeth Davis. The reporter had interviewed Mary Elisabeth, and while she did not mention Dietrich, she paid tribute to her younger brother Andrew. "He saved my life," she said, "and those of my boys. He taught me how to run the mill. I could not have done it without him after Father died in the fire."

Andrew Burnham, the article went on to state, was a teacher at a small college in Vermont, but lived most of the year in Greenleigh.

"When he heard that the mill was on fire," the article went on "Andrew Burnham rushed into the burning building to save his father and his sister's two boys, who were trapped within as they tried to rescue some of the mill's equipment. He was able to save the boys, but unfortunately could not rescue his father. He also was burned severely on his legs and one side of his body and was left with a severe limp." The article concluded with the speculation that the fire had been set by an arsonist, but that the crime had never been conclusively proven.

"Yikes," Elisabeth shuddered. She knew whom the article meant...Dietrich.

Poor Charlie! I hope your family loved you back as fiercely as you loved them.

She looked again at the photo of Charlie and his family. His face looked happy and relaxed. His wife looked pleasant enough, not too pretty but pretty enough to catch his eye, Elisabeth thought. And his children looked cheerful and unruly, even his oldest girl, Elisabeth. She appeared to be trying to escape from the sitting, and was being pulled back by a younger brother, possibly the boy who would later become Judge Burnham.

You made excellent choices, Charlie, she thought. *Every single time. I'm glad you went back after all. Even if you had to give up poetry.*

"Beth?"

It was Mum.

"Yes, Mum?"

"What are you doing up there?"

"I'm researching my paper, Mum!"

"Mrs. MacPherson has brought you some soup, she thought you must be sick because she didn't see you go to school today."

Elisabeth swallowed her laughter.

"Coming, Mum."

When she next ran into Shawn, it was at the library several days later. She was shelving books in the astronomy and space science section when she looked up to find him walking down the aisle toward her.

"Hello," she said, smiling.

"Hello," he said. "I saw that you turned in your paper."

"Are there no secrets at school?"

"It's just that I tutor American history," Shawn said, flushing. "I see everything in those classes."

"I'm teasing. I got an A."

"I heard about it. You had some amazing primary sources in there." Shawn cast her a quizzical look.

"Stuff in my attic," Elisabeth said.

"Oh, that's pretty cool." There was a moment of silence before Shawn asked, "Did you find stuff about Charlie up there?"

"I did," Elisabeth said breezily. She had already decided not to unload all of what she had learned on Shawn. She didn't want him to think she was crazy, even though he had seen Charlie with his own eyes and had heard them talk as if he were from the past.

"But it's all good," she said, determined to be vague. "He's doing fine. Wherever he is."

"Did you ever figure out how you're related?"

"Oh, we've always known how we're related," she said, again attempting to be vague. "The Davises are cousins from way back. I mean, pre-1900."

"So you're not that related."

"We are so related," she objected.

"But you're not related to the people who run the mill now."

"No, not really, but it doesn't matter. The Linfield Davises and the Greenleigh Burnhams are all over each other's family histories." It was too difficult to explain that Mary's two stepsons by Dietrich eventually took over the mill's operations, and that while they were not blood relations of the Davises, they were Mary's sons through and through.

"I see." Shawn appeared to think this over.

Elisabeth pointed to her empty cart. "I'm done."

"Great. Can I take you out?"

"Sure!" she said happily. "I would love that. Meet me by the reference desk? I have to let Mrs. Murphy know that I'm leaving."

When she emerged from the back of the stacks, zipping up her coat and donning her gloves, Shawn handed her a book.

"What's this?" she asked, surprised.

"A surprise," he said.

It looked like it had seen better days, with a worn brown cover and fragile spine. The title of the volume had rubbed off the exterior of the book.

"I had to do quite a search, but Mrs. Murphy pulled it out of storage for me. After I saw it, I felt kind of stupid. We never thought to search the stacks for Charlie. In a literal way, I mean."

Elisabeth opened it.

COLLECTED POEMS
OF
ANDREW CHARLES BURNHAM

She looked up quickly. "Wait, how did you know to search under Burnham?

"I didn't. Mrs. Murphy figured it out. Look at the dedication."

She flipped past the first couple of pages.

DEDICATED TO ELISABETH

MY GHOST OF TOMORROW

"I still don't understand," she said, her heart racing.

"The computer catalogue has all the metadata in it, including his full name. Which is Andrew Charles Davis Burnham. We searched under 'Charles Davis' and 'poetry.' And this turned up."

"He had a daughter named Elisabeth," she said quickly. "He must have dedicated this book to her."

Shawn smiled. "All right. Call it what you want. But the last poem seems right to me. I wanted you to see it."

She turned the pages until she reached the last poem.

A Ghost

There are ghosts inside of you...
Not just your own,
but the ghosts of a hundred thousand years
all piled inside.
Sometimes they are neat,
like a Russian Doll,
A stack of dishes.
They sit respectfully in your veins,
observing from the back seat,
reading over your shoulder,
ignoring their own wishes.

But sometimes they are discontent—
twisted and lumpy like laundry.
They clamor and shout,
almost bursting out of you,
pushing your skin and your bones,
banging on your cell walls,
begging for their lives back.
Begging to speak
to feel

to breathe

That is when you tell them the secret:
That you're a ghost, too.
That you're all ghosts, really,
in the eyes of time.
There is no forward or back
no beginning or end.
Only a multitude.

But you also tell them the truth:
that you are Scrooge,
the ghost of Christmas Present.
You hold the power
You are the one that speaks,
that feels,
that breathes.
You represent your current time
just as much as you do
the hundred thousand ghosts
alive inside of you.

So you say to them,
"I am the host of a hundred thousand spirits—
echoes of times long past, and people long dead.
I know sometimes you struggle,
and I know sometimes you weep,

but remember that I am a part of you,
just as you are a part of me.
Back when you were a ghost of your present,
just as I am now,
I was there, somewhere in the crowd—
though you hadn't met me yet.
And one day, I will join you, a ghost of today,
just as you are a ghost of yesterday.
And together we will watch
as the ghost of tomorrow forms.

"Wow," Elisabeth breathed.

She looked up at Shawn. He shrugged lightly.

"I don't know what it means. But it seemed right. Oh, and here." He reached into his pocket and pulled out something. He handed it to her.

It was Charlie's hat.

Elisabeth grasped it, crushed it to her chest, and bent her head to breathe deeply the scent of wood smoke and leather.

Ghost of tomorrow, she thought. You're here with me right now.

She looked up at Shawn.

"I miss him," she said.

ACKNOWLEDGMENTS

This book took so much longer than I'd expected, thanks to the unbelievable events of 2020.

Thank you to my friend, award-winning author Teri Case, for cheering me on.

And of course, Nora K. was also there for me. Every single day without fail. What would I do without you?

My fond love to this old farmhouse and the people of the past who worked hard so that today I can look out at the view and write. I have so much more to say and to thank you for.

And I especially want to thank my daughter, Grace, for her lovely poem, "A Ghost." How very strange that when I asked if you would write me a poem, you wrote the poem that was the perfect ending for my book without even knowing what my book was about! But then—maybe it's not so strange after all.

ABOUT THE AUTHOR

Maya Rushing Walker writes slow-burn, often romantic, literary fiction set in both historical and modern times, with a strong sense of place. She lives and writes in a 1780s farmhouse in northern New England, where she homeschooled four amazing young adults and was a dedicated swim and row mom. In a previous life, she was a U.S. diplomat and a Wall Street banker, and holds a B.S. in international economics from Georgetown and an A.M. in East Asian Studies from Harvard.

Find her online at mayarushingwalker.net.

facebook.com/mayarushingwalkerbooks

instagram.com/mayarushingwalker

amazon.com/author/mayarushingwalker

bookbub.com/authors/maya-rushing-walker

ALSO BY MAYA RUSHING WALKER

The Portrait

Coming Home to Greenleigh